Michael Moorcock is astonishing. His enormous output includes around fifty novels, innumerable short stories and a rock album. Born in London in 1939, he became editor of *Tarzan Adventures* at sixteen, moving on later to edit the *Sexton Blake Library*. He has earned his living as a writer/editor ever since, and is without doubt one of Britain's most popular and most prolific authors. He has been compared with Tennyson, Tolkien, Raymond Chandler, Wyndham Lewis, Ronald Firbank, Mervyn Peake, Edgar Allan Poe, Colin Wilson, Anatole France, William Burroughs, Edgar Rice Burroughs, Charles Dickens, James Joyce, Vladimir Nabokov, Jorge Luis Borges, Joyce Cary, Ray Bradbury, H. G. Wells, George Bernard Shaw and Hieronymus Bosch, among others.

'No one at the moment in England is doing more to break down the artificial divisions that have grown up in novel writing – realism, surrealism, science fiction, historical fiction, social satire, the poetic novel – than Michael Moorcock'
Angus Wilson

'He is an ingenious and energetic experimenter, restlessly original, brimming over with clever ideas'
Robert Nye, *The Guardian*

By the same author

The Cornelius Chronicles
The Final Programme
A Cure for Cancer
The English Assassin
The Condition of Muzak
*The Lives and Times of Jerry
    Cornelius*
*The Adventures of Una Persson
    and Catherine Cornelius in the
    Twentieth Century*

The Dancers at the End of Time
An Alien Heat
The Hollow Lands
The End of All Songs
*Legends from the End of
    Time*
*The Transformation of Miss
    Mavis Ming (Return of the
    Fireclown)*

Hawkmoon: The History of the
    Runestaff
The Jewel in the Skull
The Mad God's Amulet
The Sword of the Dawn
The Runestaff

Hawkmoon: The Chronicles of
    Castle Brass
Count Brass
The Champion of Garathorm
The Quest for Tanelorn

Erekosë
The Eternal Champion
Phoenix in Obsidian
The Dragon in the Sword

Elric
Elric of Melniboné
The Sailor on the Seas of Fate
The Weird of the White Wolf
The Vanishing Tower
The Bane of the Black Sword
Stormbringer
Elric at the End of Time

The Books of Corum
Tke Knight of the Swords
The Queen of the Swords
The King of the Swords
The Bull and the Spear
The Oak and the Ram
The Sword and the Stallion

Michael Kane
The City of the Beast
The Lord of the Spiders
The Masters of the Pit

The Nomad of Time
The War Lord of the Air
The Land Leviathan
The Steel Tsar

Other Titles
The Winds of Limbo
The Ice Schooner
Behold the Man
Breakfast in the Ruins
The Blood-Red Game
The Black Corridor
The Chinese Agent
The Russian Intelligence
The Distant Suns
The Rituals of Infinity
The Shores of Death
Sojan the Swordsman (juvenile)
The Golden Barge
Gloriana (or, *The Unfulfill'd
    Queene, a Romance*)
The Time Dweller
Moorcock's Book of Martyrs
    (short stories)
The Entropy Tango
Heroic Dreams (non-fiction)
Byzantium Endures
The Laughter of Carthage
The Brothel in Rosenstrasse
*The War Hound and the
    World's Pain*
The City in the Autumn Stars
Letters from Hollywood
    (non-fiction)
The Opium General
    (short stories)

MICHAEL MOORCOCK

Phoenix in Obsidian

GRAFTON BOOKS

A Division of the Collins Publishing Group

LONDON GLASGOW
TORONTO SYDNEY AUCKLAND

Grafton Books
A Division of the Collins Publishing Group
8 Grafton Street, London W1X 3LA

Published by Grafton Books 1970
Reprinted 1973, 1974, 1976, 1979, 1984, 1987

ISBN 0-583-11800-3

Printed and bound in Great Britain by
Collins, Glasgow

Set in Linotype Plantin

For Doug and Gaila Hill

PROLOGUE

A bright plain without horizons. The plain is the colour of raw, red gold. The sky is a faded purple. Two figures stand on the plain: a man and a woman. The man, dressed in dented armour, is tall with weary angular features. The woman 's beautiful—dark-haired and delicate, clad in a gown of blue silk. He is ISARDA OF TANELORN. THE WOMAN *is nameless.*

THE WOMAN

What are Time and Space but clay for the hand that holds the Cosmic Balance? This Age is moulded—that one squeezed from existence. All is flux. Lords of Law and Chaos struggle in eternal battle and neither ever completely wins or loses. The balance tilts this way and that. Time upon Time the Hand destroys its creations and begins anew. And the Earth is for ever changing. The Eternal War is the only constant in Earth's many histories, taking a multitude of forms and names.

ISARDA OF TANELORN

And the men who are involved in this struggle? Can they ever realise the true nature of their strivings?

WOMAN

Rarely.

ISARDA OF TANELORN

And will the world at length be granted rest from this state of flux?

WOMAN

We shall never know, for we shall never come face to face with the One who guides the Hand.

ISARDA

(*He spreads his arms.*) But surely some things are constant ...

WOMAN

Even the meandering river of Time can be damned or rechan-

7

nelled at the will of the Cosmic Hand. We are as uncertain of the shape of the future as we are of the validity of our reported history. Perhaps we only exist for this instant of Time? Perhaps we are immortal and will exist for ever? Nothing is known for certain, Isarda. All knowledge is illusion—purpose is a meaningless word, a mere sound, a re-assuring fragment of melody in a cacaphony of clashing chords. All is flux—matter is like these jewels. (*She throws a handful of gleaming gems upon the golden surface; they scatter. When the last jewel has ceased to move, she looks up at him.*) Sometimes they fall into a rough pattern, usually they do not. So at this moment a pattern has been formed—you and I stand here speaking. But at any moment that which constitutes our beings may be scattered again.

ISARDA

Not if we resist. Legends speak of men who forced Chaos into shape by effort of will. Aubec's hand formed your land and, indirectly, you.

WOMAN

(*Wistfully.*) Perhaps there are such men. But they go directly against the will of the One who formed them.

ISARDA

(*After a pause.*) And what if there are such men? What would become of them?

WOMAN

I do not know. But I do not envy them.

ISARDA

(*He looks away across the golden plain. He speaks softly.*) Nor I.

WOMAN

They say your city Tanelorn is eternal. They say that because of a Hero's will she has existed through every transformation of the Earth. They say that even the most haunted of folk find peace there.

ISARDA

It is also said that they must first have a will for peace before they can find Tanelorn.

8

WOMAN

(*Bowing her head.*) And few have that.

—The Chronicle of the Black Sword
(Vol. 1008 Scr. 14: *Isarda's Reckoning*)

BOOK ONE

Premonitions

But yesternight I pray'd aloud
In anguish and in agony,
Up-starting from the fiendish crowd
Of shapes and thoughts that tortured me:
A lurid light, a trampling throng,
Sense of intolerable wrong,
And whom I scorned, those only strong!
Thirst of revenge, the powerless will
Still baffled, and yet burning still!
Desire with loathing strangely mixed
On wild or hateful objects fixed.
Fantastic passions! Maddening brawl!
And shame and terror over all!
Deeds to be hid which were not hid,
Which all confused I could not know
Whether I suffered, or I did:
For all seem'd guilt, remorse or woe,
My own or others still the same
Life-stifling fear, soul-stifling shame.
                    S. T. Coleridge: *The Pains of Sleep*

CHAPTER ONE

OF AN EARTH REBORN

I know grief and I know love and I think I know what death may be, though it is said I am immortal. I have been told I have a destiny, but what that is, save for ever to be moved by the tides of chance, to perform miserable deeds, I do not know.

I was called John Daker and perhaps many other names. Then I was called Erekosë, the Eternal Champion, and I slew the human race because it had betrayed what I considered to be my ideals, because I loved a woman of another race, a race I

11

thought nobler and which was called the Eldren. The woman was called Ermizhad and she could never bear me children.

And, having slain my race, I was happy.

With Ermizhad and her brother Arjavh I ruled the Eldren, that graceful people which had existed on Earth well before mankind had come to disrupt its harmony.

The dreams, which had beset my sleeping hours when I had first come to this world, were now rare and hardly remembered at all on waking. Once they had terrified me, made me think that I must be insane. I had experienced fragments of a million incarnations, always as some sort of warrior; I had not known which identity was my 'true' one. Torn by divided loyalties, by the stresses in my own brain, I had been mad for a while, of this I was now sure.

But I was mad no longer and I committed myself to restoring the beauty I had destroyed in my warrings—first as the Champion of one side, then of the other—over the Earth.

Where armies had marched we planted shrubs and flowers. Where cities had been we made forests grow. And the Earth became gentle, calm and beautiful.

And my love for Ermizhad did not wain.

It grew. It developed so that I loved each new facet I discovered in her character.

The Earth became harmonious. And Erekosë, the Eternal Champion, and Ermizhad, Paramount Princess of the Eldren, reflected that harmony.

The great, terrifying weapons which we had used to overcome mankind were sealed away, and we swore that we should never use them again.

The Eldren cities, razed by the Marshals of Humanity when I had led them, were restored, and soon Eldren children sang in their streets, flowering shrubs bloomed on their balconies and terraces. Green turf grew over the scars cut with the swords of mankind's paladins. And the Eldren forgot the men who had once sought to destroy their race.

Only I remembered, for mankind had called me to lead them against the Eldren. Instead I had betrayed mankind—every man, woman and child had died because of me. The Droonaa River had flowed with their blood. Now it flowed with sweet water. But the water could not wash away the guilt that would sometimes consume me.

And yet I was happy. It seemed to me that I had never known such peace of soul, such tranquillity of mind.

Ermizhad and I would wander about the walls and terraces of Loos Ptokai, the Eldren capital, and we never tired of each other's company. Sometimes we would discuss a fine point of philosophy, at other times we were content to sit in silence, breathing in the rich and delicate scents of a garden.

And when the mood took us, we would embark upon a slender Eldren ship and sail about the world to witness its wonders— the Plains of Melting Ice, the Mountains of Sorrow, the mighty forests and gentle hills, the rolling plains of the two continents once inhabited by mankind, Necralala and Zavara. But then, sometimes, a mood of melancholy would sweep over me and we would set sail again for the third continent, the Southern continent called Mernadin, where the Eldren had lived since ancient times.

It was at these times that Ermizhad would comfort me, soothing away my memories and my shame.

'You know that I believe all this was pre-ordained,' she would say. Her cool, soft hands would stroke my brow. 'Mankind's purpose was to destroy our race. This ambition destroyed them. You were merely the instrument of their destruction.'

'And yet,' I would reply, 'have I no freewill? Was the only solution the genocide I committed? I had hoped that mankind and the Eldren could live in peace...'

'And you tried to bring such a thing to pass. But they would have none of it. They tried to destroy you as they tried to destroy the Eldren. They almost succeeded. Do not forget that, Erekosë. They almost succeeded.'

'Sometimes,' I would confide, 'I wish that I were back in the world of John Daker. I once thought that world overly complicated and stifling. But now I realise that every world contains the same factors I hated, if in a different form. The Cycles of Time may change, Ermizhad, but the human condition does not. It was that condition I hoped to change. I failed. Perhaps that is my destiny—to strive to change the very nature of humanity—and fail...'

But Ermizhad was not human and, while she could sympathise and guess at what I meant, she could not understand. It was the one thing she could not understand.

'Your kind had many virtues,' she would say. Then she would pause and frown and be unable to complete her statement.

'Aye, but their very virtues became their vices. It was ever thus with mankind. A young man hating poverty and squalor would seek to change it by destroying something that was beautiful. Seeing people dying in misery, he would kill others. Seeing starvation, he would burn crops. Hating tyranny, he would give himself body and soul to that great tyrant War. Hating disorder, he would invent devices that brought further chaos. Loving peace, he would repress learning, outlaw art, cause conflict. The history of the human race was one prolonged tragedy, Ermizhad.'

And Ermizhad would kiss me lightly. 'And now the tragedy is ended.'

'So it seems, for the Eldren know how to live in tranquillity and retain their vitality. Yet sometimes I feel that the tragedy is still being played—perhaps played a thousand times in different guises. And the tragedy requires its principal actors. Perhaps I am one such. Perhaps I shall be called again to play my role. Perhaps my life with you is merely a pause between scenes...'

And to this statement she could offer no reply, save to take me in her arms and bring me the comfort of her sweet lips.

Gaily coloured birds and graceful beasts played where mankind had once raised its cities and beaten its battle-drums, but within those new-born forests and on the grass of those fresh-healed hills there were ghosts. The ghosts of Iolinda, who had loved me, of her father, the weak king Rigenos, who had sought my help, of Count Roldero, kindly Grand Marshal of Humanity, of all the others who had died because of me.

Yet it had been no choice of my own to come to this world, to take up the sword of Erekosë, the Eternal Champion, to put on Erekosë's armour, to ride at the head of a bright army as mankind's chief paladin, to learn that the Eldren were not the Hounds of Evil which King Rigenos had described, that they were, in fact, the victims of mankind's insensate hatred...

No choice of my own...

At root, that was the phrase most often haunting my moods of melancholy.

Yet those moods came more rarely as the years rolled by and Ermizhad and I did not age and continued to feel the same passion we had felt at our first meeting.

They were years of laughter, fine conversation, ecstasy, beauty, affection. One year blended into another until a hundred or so had passed.

Then the Ghost Worlds—those strange worlds which shifted through Time and Space at an angle to the rest of the universe we knew—came again in conjunction with the Earth.

CHAPTER TWO

OF A GROWING DOOM

Ermizhad's brother was Prince Arjavh. Handsome, in the manner of the slender Eldren, with a pointed golden face and slanting eyes that were milky and blue-flecked, Arjavh had as much affection for me as I had for him. His wit and his wisdom had often inspired me and he was for ever laughing.

So it was that I was surprised one day to visit him in his laboratory and find him frowning.

He looked up from his sheets of calculations and tried to alter his expression, but I could tell he was concerned—perhaps about some discovery he had made in his researches.

'What is it, Arjavh?' I asked lightly. 'Those look to me like astronomical charts. Is a comet on course for Loos Ptokai? Must we all evacuate the city?'

He smiled and shook his head. 'Nothing so simple. Perhaps not as dramatic, either. I am not sure there is anything to fear, but we would do well to be prepared, for it seems the Ghost Worlds are about to touch ours again.'

'But the Ghost Worlds offer the Eldren no harm, surely. You have summoned allies from them in the past.'

'True. Yet the last time the Ghost Worlds were in conjunction with Earth—that was the time you came here. Possibly it was coincidental. Possibly you are from one of the Ghost Worlds and that is how it was in Rigenos's power to call you.'

I frowned. 'I understand your concern. It is for me.'

Arjavh nodded his head and said nothing.

'Some say Humanity came originally from the Ghost Worlds, do they not?' I gave him a direct look.

'Aye.'

'Have you any specific fears on my behalf?' I asked him.

He sighed. 'No. Though the Eldren invented a means of bridging the dimensions between our Earth and the Ghost Worlds, we never explored them. Our visits could, of necessity, only be brief and our contact was with those dwellers in the Ghost Worlds who were kin to the Eldren.'

'Do you fear that I will be recalled to the world I left?' I became tense. I could not bear the thought of being parted from Ermizhad, from the tranquil world of the Eldren.

'I do not know, Erekosë.'

Was I to become John Daker again?

Though I only dimly remembered my life in that era I for some reason called the Twentieth Century, I knew that I had not felt at ease there, that there had been within me an intense dissatisfaction with my life and circumstances. My naturally passionate and romantic disposition (which I did not regard as a virtue, for it had led me to commit the deeds I have already recounted) had been repressed by my surroundings, by my society and by the work I had done to make a living. I had felt more out of place there, among my own kind, than I did living here with an alien race. I felt that it might be better to kill myself, rather than return to John Daker's world, perhaps without even the memory of this one.

On the other hand, the Ghost Worlds might be nothing to do with me. They might belong to a universe which had never been inhabited by men (though the Eldren researches did not suggest this).

'Is there nothing else we can discover?' I asked Prince Arjavh.

'I am continuing my investigations. It is all I can do.'

Gloomily, I left his laboratory and returned to the chambers where Ermizhad awaited me. We had planned to ride out over the familiar fields surroundings Loos Ptokai, but now I told her that I did not feel like riding.

Noting my mood, she said: 'Are you remembering what passed a century ago, Erekosë?'

I shook my head. Then I told her what Arjavh had said.

She, too, became thoughtful. 'It was probably a coincidence,' she said. But there was little conviction in her tone. There was a trace of fear in her eye when she looked up at me.

I took her in my arms.

'I should die, I think, if you were taken from me, Erekosë,' she said.

My lips were dry, my throat tight. 'If I were taken,' I told her, 'I would spend eternity in finding you again. And I would find you again, Ermizhad.'

When she spoke next, it was almost in astonishment. 'Is your love for me that strong, Erekosë?'

'It is stronger, Ermizhad.'

She drew away from me, holding my hands in hers. Those hands, hers and mine, were trembling. She tried to smile, to banish the premonitions filling her, but she could not.

'Why, then,' she said, 'there is nothing at all to fear!'

But that night, as I slept beside her, the dreams which I had experienced as John Daker, which had plagued me in my first year on this new world, began to creep back into the caverns of my mind.

First there were no images. Only names. A long list of names chanted in a booming voice that seemed to have a trace of mockery in it.

Corum Jhaelen Irsei. Konrad Arflane. Asquiol of Pompei. Urlik Skarsol. Aubec of Kaneloon. Shaleen. Artos. Alerik. Erekosë...

I tried to stop the voice there. I tried to shout, to say that I was Erekosë—only Erekosë. But I could not speak.

The roll continued:

Ryan. Hawkmoon. Powys. Cornell. Brian. Umpata. Sojan. Klan. Clovis Marca. Pournachas. Oshbek-Uy. Ulysses. Ilanth.

My own voice came now:

'NO! I AM ONLY EREKOSE.'   Ü Ü Ü

'Champion Eternal. Fate's Soldier.'

'NO!'

Elric. Ilanth. Mejink-La-Kos. Cornelius.

'NO! NO! I AM WEARY. I CAN WAR NO MORE!'

The sword. The armour. The battle banners. Fire. Death. Ruin.

'NO!'

'Erekosë!'

'YES! YES!'

I was screaming. I was sweating. I was sitting upright in the bed.

And it was Ermizhad's voice that was calling my name now. Panting, I fell back on to the pillows, into her arms.

'The dreams have returned,' she said.

'They have returned.'

I lay my head upon her breast and I wept.

'This means nothing,' she said. 'It was only a nightmare. You fear that you will be recalled and your own mind gives substance to that fear. That is all.'

'Is it, Ermizhad?'

She stroked my head.

I looked up and saw her face through the darkness. It was strained. There were tears in her blue-flecked eyes.

'Is it?'

'Yes, my love. Yes.'

But I knew that the same sense of doom that lay upon my heart now lay upon hers.

We slept no more that night.

CHAPTER THREE

OF A VISITATION

Next morning I went straight to Prince Arjavh's laboratory and told him of the voice that had come to me in my sleep.

It was plain that he was distressed and plain also that he felt impotent to help me.

'If the voice was a mere nightmare—and I agree that it might be—then I could give you a potion to ensure dreamless sleep,' he said.

'And if not?'

'There is no way I can protect you.'

'Then the voice could be calling from the Ghost Worlds?'

'Even that is not certain. It could be that the information I gave you yesterday merely triggered some empathatic impulse in your own brain—which allowed this "voice" to make contact with you again. Perhaps the tranquillity you have known here made it impossible for you to be reached. Now that your brain is again in torment, then whatever it is that seeks to speak to you might now be able to do so.'

'These suppositions do not ease my mind,' I said bitterly.

'I know they do not, Erekosë. Would that you had never come to my laboratory and learned of the Ghost Worlds. I should have kept this from you.'

'It would have made no difference, Arjavh.'

'Who knows?'

I stretched out my hand. 'Give me the potion of which you spoke. At least we'll be able to put the theory to the test—that my own brain conjures this mocking voice.'

He went to a chest of glowing crystal and opened the lid, taking a small leather bag from it.

'Pour this powder into a goblet of wine tonight and drink all down.'

'Thank you,' I said as I took the bag.

He paused before he spoke again. 'Erekosë, if you are called

18

from us, we shall waste no time in trying to find you. You are loved by all the Eldren and we would not lose you. If, somewhere in those unimaginable regions of Time and Space, you can be found—we shall find you.'

I was a little comforted by this assurance. Yet the speech was too much like a leave-taking for me to like it greatly. It was as if Arjavh had already accepted that I would be going.

Ermizhad and I spent the rest of that day walking hand in hand among the bowers of the palace garden. We spoke little, but gripped each other tightly and hardly dared look into each other's eyes for fear of the grief which would be mirrored there.

From hidden galleries came the intricate melodies of the great Eldren composers, played by musicians placed there by Prince Arjavh. The music was sweet, monumental, harmonious. To some degree it eased the dread that filled my brain.

A golden sun, huge and warm, hung in a pale blue sky. It shone its rays on delicately scented flowers in a multitude of hues, on vines and trees, on the white walls of the gardens.

We climbed the walls and looked out over the gentle hills and plains of the Southern continent. A herd of deer were grazing. Birds sailed lazily in the sky.

I could not leave all this beauty to return to the noise and the filth of the world I had left, to the sad existence of John Daker.

Evening came and the air was filled with birdsong and the heavier perfume of the flowers. Slowly we walked back to the palace. Tightly we held each other's hands.

Like a condemned man, I mounted the steps that led to our chambers. Disrobing myself, I wondered if I should ever wear such clothes again. Lying down upon the bed while Ermizhad prepared the sleeping draught, I prayed that I should not rise next morning in the apartment in the city where John Daker had lived.

I stared up at the fluted ceiling of the chamber, looked around at the bright wall-hangings, the vases of flowers, the finely wrought furnishings, and I attempted to fix all this in my mind, just as I had already fixed Ermizhad's face.

She brought me the drink. I looked deep into her tear-filled eyes and drank.

It was a parting. A parting we dare not admit.

Almost immediately I sank into a heavy slumber and it seemed to me at that moment that perhaps Ermizhad and Arjavh had been right and that the voice was simply a manifestation of my unease.

I do not know at what hour I was disturbed in that deep, drugged sleep. I was barely conscious. My brain seemed swaddled in fold upon fold of dark velvet, but muffled, and as if from far off, I faintly heard the voice again.

I could make out no words this time and I believe I smiled to myself, feeling relief that the drug was guarding me from that which sought to call me away. The voice became more urgent, but I could ignore it. I stirred and reached out for Ermizhad, throwing one arm across her slumbering body.

Still the voice called. Still I ignored it. Now I felt that if I could last this night, the voice would cease its attempt to recall me. I would know that I could not be drawn away so easily from the world where I had found love and tranquillity.

The voice faded and I slept on, with Ermizhad in my arms, with hope in my heart.

The voice returned some time later, but still I could ignore it.

Then the voice apparently ceased altogether and I sank again into my heavy sleep.

I think it must have been an hour or two before dawn that I heard a noise not within my head but in the room. Thinking that Ermizhad must have arisen, I opened my eyes. It was dark. I saw nothing. But Ermizhad was beside me. Then I heard the noise again. It was like the slap of a scabbarded sword against an armoured leg. I sat upright. My eyes were clogged with sleep, my head felt muzzy under the effects of the drug. I peered drowsily about the room.

And then I saw the figure who stood there.

'Who are you?' I asked, rather querulously. Maybe it was some servant? In Loos Ptokai there were no thieves, no threats of assassination.

The figure did not answer. It seemed to be staring at me. Gradually I distinguished more details and then I knew that this was no Eldren.

The figure had a barbaric appearance, though its apparel was rich and finely made. It wore a huge, grotesque helmet which completely framed a heavily bearded face. On its broad chest was a metal breastplate, as intricately ornamented as the helm. Over this was a thick, sleeveless coat of what appeared to be sheepskin. On his legs were britches that were probably of lacquered hide, black and with sinuous designs picked out in gold and silver. Greaves on his legs matched the breastplate and his feet were encased in boots of the same shaggy, white pelt as his long coat. On his hip was a sword.

The figure did not move, but continued to regard me from the shadow cast by the peak of the grotesque helmet. The eyes were visible now. They burned. They were urgent.

This was no human of this world, no follower of King Rigenos who had somehow escaped the vengeance I had brought. A faint recollection came and went. But the garb was not that of any period of history I could remember from my life as John Daker.

Was this a visitor from the Ghost Worlds?

If so, his appearance was very different from that of the other Ghost Worlds dwellers who had once helped Ermizhad when she was a prisoner of King Rigenos.

I repeated my question.

'Who are you?'

The figure tried to speak but plainly could not.

He raised both hands to his head. He removed his helmet. He brushed back black, long hair from his face. He moved nearer to the window.

The face was familiar.

It was my own.

I shrank back in the bed. Never before had I felt such complete terror. I do not think I have felt it since.

'What do you want?' I screamed. 'What do you want?'

In some other part of my churning brain I seem to remember wondering why Ermizhad did not awake but continued to sleep peacefully at my side.

The figure's mouth moved as if he was speaking, but I heard no words.

Was this a nightmare induced by the drug? If so, I think I should have preferred the voice.

'Get out of here! Begone!'

The visitation made several gestures which I could not interpret. Again its mouth moved, but no words reached me.

Screaming, I leapt from the bed and rushed at the figure which bore my face. But it moved away, a puzzled expression on its features.

There were no swords now in the Eldren palace, or I would have found one and used it against the figure. I think I had some mindless scheme to grasp his sword and use it against him.

'Begone! Begone!'

Then I tripped, fell scrabbling on the flagstones of the bed-chamber, shaking still with terror, screaming at the apparition which continued to look down at me. I rose again, tottered and was falling, falling, falling...

And as I fell, the voice filled my ears once again. It was full of triumphant joy.

'URLIK,' *it cried.* 'URLIK SKARSOL! URLIK! UR-LIK! ICE-HERO, COME TO US!'

'I WILL NOT!'

But now I did not deny that the name was mine. I tried to refuse the one or ones who called it. As I whirled and tumbled through the corridors of eternity, I sought to fling myself back—back to Ermizhad and the world of the Eldren.

'URLIK SKARSOL! COUNT OF THE WHITE WASTES! LORD OF THE FROZEN KEEP! PRINCE OF THE SOUTHERN ICE! MASTER OF THE COLD SWORD! HE WILL COME IN FURS AND METAL, HIS CHARIOT DRAWN BY BEARS, HIS BLACK BEARD BRISTLING, TO CLAIM HIS BLADE, TO AID HIS FOLK!'

'I WILL GIVE YOU NO AID! I DESIRE NO BLADE! LET ME SLEEP! I BEG YOU—LET ME SLEEP!'

'AWAKE, URLIK SKARSOL. THE PROPHECY DE-MANDS IT!'

Now fragments of a vision came to me. I saw cities carved from cliffs of volcanic rock—obsidian and moody, built on the shores of sluggish seas, beneath dark, livid skies. I saw a sea that was like grey marble veined with black and I realised it was a sea on which floated great ice-floes.

The vision filled me with grief—not because it was strange and unfamiliar, but because it was familiar.

I knew for certain then that, weary with war, I had been called to fight yet another fight...

BOOK TWO

The Champion's Road

The Warriors are in Silver,
The Citizens in Silk.
In Brazen Car the Champion rides,
A Hero clad in Grief.
                    —The Chronicle of the Black Sword

CHAPTER ONE

THE ICE WASTES

I was still travelling, but it was no longer as if I had been tugged down into a maelstrom. I was moving slowly forward, though I was not moving my legs.

My vision cleared. The scene before me was concrete enough, though scarcely reassuring. I clung to a wisp of hope that I was still dreaming, but everything in me told me that this was not so. Just as John Daker had been called against his will to the world of the Eldren, so had Erekosë been called to this world.

And I knew my name. It had been repeated often enough. But I knew it as if it had always been mine. I was Urlik Skarsol of the South Ice.

The scene before me confirmed it, for I stared across a world of ice. It came to me that I had seen other ice plains in other incarnations, but this one I recognised for what it was. I was travelling over a dying planet. And in the sky above me was a small, dim red sun—a dying sun. That the world was Earth, I was certain, but it was an Earth at the end of its cycle. John Daker would have seen it as being in his distant future, but I had long-since ceased to make easy definitions of 'past' and 'future'. If Time were my enemy, then she was an enemy without face or form; an enemy I could not see; an enemy I could not fight.

I was travelling in a chariot which seemed fashioned of silver and bronze, its heavy decoration reminiscent of the decoration I had seen on the armour of my voiceless visitor. Its four great iron-shod wheels had been bolted to skis apparently made of polished ebony. In the shafts at the front were the four creatures which dragged the chariot over the ice. The creatures were larger, longer-legged variations of the polar bears which had existed on John Daker's world. They loped at a regular and surprisingly rapid speed. I stood upright in the chariot, holding their reins. Before me was a chest designed to fit the space. It seemed made of some hard wood overlaid with silver, its corners strengthened with strips of iron. It had a great iron lock and handle at the centre of the lid and the whole chest was decorated in black, brown and blue enamel work depicting dragons, warriors, trees and flowers, all flowing and intertwining. There were strange, flowing runes picked out around the lock and I was surprised that I could read them easily: *This is the chest of Count Urlik Skarsol, Lord of the Frozen Keep.* On the right of the chest three heavy rings had been soldered to the side of the chariot and through the rings was placed the silver- and brass-shod haft of a lance which must have been at least seven feet long, ending in a huge, cruelly barbed head of gleaming iron. On the other side of the chest was a weapon whose haft was the twin to the spear's, but whose head was that of a great, broad-bladed axe, as beautifully decorated as the trunk, with delicately engraved designs. I felt at my belt. There was no sword there, only a pouch and, on my right hip, a key. I unhooked the key from my belt and looked at it curiously. I bent and inserted it with some difficulty (for the chariot had a tendency to lurch on the rough ice) opened the trunk, expecting to find a sword there.

But there was no sword, only provisions, spare clothing and the like—the things a man would take with him if he were making a long journey.

I smiled despairingly. I had made a very long journey. I closed the chest and locked it, replacing the key on my belt.

And then I noticed what I was wearing. I had a heavily decorated iron breastplate, a huge coat of thick, coarse wool, a leather jerkin, breeks of lacquered leather, greaves of the same design as the breastplate, boots apparently of the same sheepskin-like stuff as the coat. I reached up to my head and touched metal. I ran my fingers over the serpentine designs which had been raised on the helmet.

With a growing sense of terror I moved my hands to my face.

Its contours were familiar enough, but there was now a thick moustache on my upper lip, a great crop of black whiskers on my chin.

I had seen a hand-mirror in the chest. I seized the key, unlocked the bolt, flung back the lid, rummaged until I found the mirror which was of highly polished silver and not glass. I hesitated for a moment and then forced my hand to raise the mirror to my face.

I saw the face and helmet of my visitor—of the apparition which had come to me in the night.

I was now that apparition.

With a moan, with a sense of foreboding in my heart which I was unable to vocalise, I dropped the mirror back into the chest and slammed the lid shut. My hand went out to grip the haft of the tall lance and I clung to it, thought I must snap it with the force I applied.

And here I was on the pale ice beneath a darkling sky, alone and in torment, cut off from the one woman who had brought me tranquillity of spirit, the one world where I had felt free and at peace. I felt as a man must feel who has been in the grip of uncontrollable madness, thinks he is cured and then finds himself once again seized by the horrible insanity of which he thought himself purged.

I opened my mouth and I cried out against the ice. The breath steamed from my lips and boiled in the air like ectoplasm, writhed as if imitating the agony of spirit that was within me. I shook my fist at the dim, red, far-away globe that was this world's sun.

And all the while the white bears loped on, dragging me and my chariot to an unknown destination.

'Ermizhad!' I cried. 'Ermizhad!'

I wondered if somewhere she would hear me, call me as that other voice had called me.

'Ermizhad!'

But the dark sky was silent, the gloomy ice was still, the sun looked down like the eye of an old, old, senile man, uncomprehending.

On and on ran the tireless bears; on, across the perpetual ice; on, through perpetual twilight. On and on, while I wept and moaned and shrieked and at last was quiet, standing in my lurching chariot as if I, too, were made of ice.

I knew that, for the moment, I must accept my fate, discover where the bears were taking me, hope that when I reached my destination I would be able to dicover a means of going back to the Eldren world, of finding my Ermizhad again.

I knew the hope was a faint one, but I clung to it as I had clung to the shaft of the spear. It was all I had. But where she was in the universe—in a host of alternate universes if the Eldren theories were right—I had no idea. Neither did I know where this world was. While it might be one of the Ghost Worlds and therefore possible for Eldren expeditions to reach, it could as easily be some other Earth, sundered by aeons from the world I had grown to love and to think of as my own.

But now I was again the Eternal Champion, summoned, no doubt, to fight in some cause with which I had scant sympathy, by a people who could easily be as wretched and self-deceiving as those who had been ruled by King Rigenos.

Why should I be singled out for this everlasting task? Why was I to be allowed no permanent peace?

Again my thoughts turned to the possibility that I had been responsible, in some incarnation, of a cosmic crime, so terrible that it was my fate to be swept back and forth across eternity. But what that crime could be that it deserved so frightful a punishment, I could not guess.

It seemed to grow colder. I reached into the chest and knew I should find gauntlets there. I drew the gloves on to my hands, wrapped the heavy coat more tightly about me, sat down on the chest, still holding the reins, and sank into a doze which I hoped would heal, at least a little, my wounded brain.

And still we drove over ice. Thousands of miles of ice. Had this world grown so old and cold that now there was nothing but ice from pole to pole?

Soon, I hoped, I would find out.

CHAPTER TWO

THE OBSIDIAN CITY

Across the timeless ice, beneath the waning sun, I moved in my chariot of bronze and silver. The long-limbed white bears only rarely slowed and never stopped. It was as if they, like me, were possessed of some force they could not control. Rusty clouds crossed the sky occasionally—slow ships on a livid sea—but there was nothing to mark the passing of the hours for the sun itself was frozen in the sky and the faint stars which gleamed behind it were arranged in constellations which were only vaguely familiar. It came to me then that the globe itself had apparently ceased to spin or, if it moved at all, moved so gradually as not to be apparent to a man without the necessary measuring instruments.

I reflected bitterly that the landscape certainly matched my mood, probably even exacerbated it.

Then, through the gloom, I thought I saw something which relieved the monotony of ice which hitherto had lain on all sides. Perhaps it was nothing more than a band of low cloud, but I kept my gaze fixed hopefully upon it and, as the bears drew closer, saw that these were the dark shapes of mountains apparently rising out of the ice plain. Were they mountains of ice and nothing more? Or were they of rock, indicating that not all the planet was covered by ice?

I had never seen such jagged crags. Despondently I concluded that they must be made of ice shaped by wind and time into such peculiar serrations.

But then, as we drew yet closer, I remembered the vision I had had when I was dragged away from Ermizhad's side. Now it seemed these were, indeed, rocks—volcanic rocks with a glassy lustre. Colours became apparent—deep greens and browns and blacks.

I shouted to the bears and jerked the reins to make them go faster.

And I discovered that I knew their names.

'Ho, Snarler! Ho, Render! Ho, Growler! Ho, Longclaw! Faster!'

They leaned in their harness and their speed increased. The chariot lurched and jogged and skipped over the rough ice.

'Faster!'

I had been right. Now I could see that the ice gave way to rock that was, if anything, smoother than glass. The ice thinned and then the chariot was bumping on to the rock that formed the foothills of the mountain range which now flung its spiky peaks into a mass of low, rust-coloured clouds, where they were lost to my view.

These were high and gloomy peaks. They dominated me, seemed to threaten me, and they were certainly no comfort to the eye. But they offered me some hope, particularly as I made out what could be a pass between two tall cliffs.

The range seemed principally a mixture of basalt and obsidian and on both sides of me now were huge boulders between which passed a natural causeway down which I drove my straining bears. I could see the strangely coloured clouds clinging to the upper slopes of the cliffs, almost as smoke clings to oil.

And now, as I discerned more detail, I could only gasp at the wonder of the cliffs. That they were volcanic in origin there was no doubt, for the spiky upper peaks were plainly of pumice, while the lower flanks were either of black, green or purple obsidian, smooth and shiny, or basalt which had formed into something not unlike the delicately fluted columns of fine Gothic architecture. They could almost have been built by some intelligence possessed of gigantic size. Elsewhere the basalt was red and deep blue and cellular in appearance, almost like coral. In other places the same rock was a more familiar coal black and dark grey. And at still more levels there were veins of iridescent rock that caught what little light there was and were as richly coloured as the feathers of a peacock.

I guessed that this region must have resisted the march of the ice because it had been the last volcanically active region on the planet.

Now I had entered the pass. It was narrow and the cliffs seemed as if they were about to crush me. Some parts of them were pitted with caves which my fancy saw as malicious eyes staring down at me. I kept a firm grip on my lance as I drove. For all my imaginings, there was always the chance that there were real dangers here from beasts which might inhabit the caves.

The pass wound around the bases of many mountains, all of the same strange formations and colours. The ground became less level and the bears had great difficulty pulling the chariot. At last, though I had no inclination to stop in that gloomy pass, I drew rein and dismounted from the chariot, inspecting the runners and the bolts attaching them to the wheels. I knew instinctively that I had the appropriate tools in my chest and I opened the lid and eventually discovered them in a box of the same design and manufacture as the chest itself.

With some effort I unbolted the runners and slid them into lugs running along the side of the chariot.

Just as I had discovered, as Erekosë, that I had an instinctive skill with weapons and horses, that I knew every piece of armour as if I had always worn it, now I found that the work-ings of this chariot were completely familiar to me.

With the wheels free, the chariot moved much faster, though it was even more difficult to keep my balance than before.

Many hours must have passed before I rounded a curve in the pass and saw that I had come to the other side of the mountain range.

Smooth rock sloped down to a crystalline beach. And against the beach moved the sluggish tide of an almost viscous sea.

Elsewhere the mountains entered the sea itself and I could see jagged peaks jutting out of the water which must have con-tained a much greater quantity of salt than even the Dead Sea of John Daker's world. The low, brown clouds seemed to meet the sea only a short distance out. The dark crystals of the beach were devoid of plant life and here even the faint light from the small, red sun barely pierced the darkness.

It was as if I had come to the edge of the world at the end of time.

I could not believe that anything lived here—whether man, plant or beast.

But now the bears had reached the beach and the wheels crunched on the crystal and the creatures did not stop, but turned sharply towards the East, dragging me and the chariot along the shore of that dark and morbid ocean.

Though it was warmer here than it had been on the ice, I shuddered. Again my imagination took an unpleasant turn as I guessed at what kind of monsters might dwell beneath the sur-face of the twilit sea, what kind of people could bear to live beside it.

I was soon to have my answer—or, at least, part of it—when through the gloom I heard the sound of human voices and soon saw those who had uttered the voices.

They rode huge animals which moved not on legs but on strong, muscular flippers and whose bodies sloped sharply back to end in wide tails which balanced them. In some astonishment I realised that these riding beasts had been, at some earlier period of their evolution, sea-lions. They still had the dog-like, whiskered faces, the huge, staring eyes. The saddles on their backs had been built up so that the rider sat almost level. Each rider held a rod of some kind which issued a faint glow in the darkness.

But were the riders human? Their bodies, encased in ornate

armour, were bulbous and, in comparison, their arms and legs were sticklike, their heads—also enclosed in helmets—tiny. They had swords, lances and axes at their hips or in sheaths attached to their saddles. From within their visors their voices boomed and were echoed by the lowering cliffs, but I could distinguish no words.

They rode their seal-beasts skilfully along the shores of the salt-thick sea until they were only a few yards from me. Then they stopped.

In turn, I stopped my chariot.

A silence fell. I placed my hand upon the shaft of my tall spear while my bears moved restlessly in their harness.

I inspected them more closely. They were somewhat froglike in appearance, if the armour actually displayed the basic shapes of their bodies. The accoutrements and armour was so ornate and, to my taste, over-worked, that it was almost impossible to pick out individual designs. Most of the suits were of a reddish gold in colour, though glowing greens and yellows became apparent in the light from their dim torches.

After some moments in which they made no further effort to communicate with me I decided to speak.

'Are you those who called me?' I asked.

Visors turned, gestures were made, but they did not reply.

'What people are you?' I said. 'Do you recognise me?'

This time a few words passed between the riders but they still did not speak directly to me. They urged their beasts into a wide semicircle and then surrounded me. I kept my hand firmly on the shaft of my lance.

'I am Urlik Skarsol,' I said. 'Did you not summon me?'

Now one spoke, his voice muffled in his helm. 'We did not summon you, Urlik Skarsol. But we know your name and bid you be our guest in Rowernarc.' He gestured with his torch in the direction from which they had come. 'We are Bishop Bephig's men. He would wish us to make you welcome.'

'I accept your hospitality.'

There had been respect in the speaker's voice after he had heard my name, but I was surprised that he had not been expecting me. Why had the bears brought me here? Where else was there to go, save beyond the sea? And it seemed to me that beyond the sea lay nothing but limbo. I could imagine those sluggish waters dripping over the edge of the world into the total blackness of the cosmic void.

I allowed them to escort me along the beach until it curved

into a bay, at the end of which was a steep, high cliff up which climbed a number of paths, evidently cut by men. These paths led to the mouths of archways as heavily ornamented as the armour worn by the riders. High above, the most distant archways were half hidden by the thick, brown clouds clinging to the rock.

This was not merely a village of cliff-dwellers. Judging by the sophistication of the ornament, it was a great city, carved from the gleaming obsidian.

'That is Rowernarc,' said the rider nearest me. 'Rowernarc—the Obsidian City.'

CHAPTER THREE

THE LORD SPIRITUAL

The paths up to the yawning gateways in the cliff-face were wide enough to take my chariot. Somewhat reluctantly the bears began to climb.

The froglike riders led the way, ascending higher and higher along the obsidian causeways, passing several baroque arches festooned with gargoyles which, while being of exquisite workmanship, were the products of dark and morbid brains.

I looked towards the gloomy bay, at the low, brown clouds, at the heavy, unnatural sea, and it seemed for a moment that all this world was enclosed in one murky cave—in one cold hell.

And if the landscape reminded me of Hell, then subsequent events were soon to confirm my impression.

Eventually we reached an archway of particularly heavy decoration—all carved from the multicoloured living obsidian—and the strange seal-beasts turned and stopped and thwacked their forefins on the ground in a complicated rhythm.

Within the shadow of the arch I could now detect a barrier. It seemed to be a door—but a door that was made of solid porphyritic rock from which all kinds of strange beasts and half-human creatures had been carved. Whether these representations, too, were the inventions of near-crazed minds or whether they were taken from types actually to be found in this world, I could not tell. But some of the designs were loathsome and I avoided looking at them as much as possible.

In answer to the strange signal of the seals, this door began to

31

scrape backwards—the whole block moving into the cavern behind it—to allow us passage around it. My chariot wheel caught on one edge and I was forced to manoeuvre for a moment before I could pass into the chamber.

This chamber was poorly lit by the same staffs of faint artificial light which the riders had carried. The staffs reminded me of battery-operated electric torches which needed recharging. Somehow I thought that these could not be recharged. I had the feeling that as the artificial brands died, so a little more light vanished from this world. It would not be long, I thought, before all the brands were extinguished.

The froglike riders were dismounting, handing their beasts over to grooms who, to my relief, looked ordinarily human, though pale and somewhat scrawny. These grooms were dressed in smocks bearing a complicated piece of embroidered insignia which again was so complex as to have no indication to me what it was meant to represent. I suddenly had an insight into the lives of these people. Living in their rock cities on a dying planet, surrounded by bleak ice and gloomy seas, they whiled away their days at various crafts, adding embellishment upon complicated embellishment, producing work which was so introverted that it doubtless lost its meaning even to them. It was the art of a decaying race and yet, ironically, it would outlast them by centuries, perhaps for ever when the atmosphere eventually disappeared.

I felt a reluctance to deliver my chariot and its weapons over to the grooms, but there was little else I could do. Seal-beasts and chariot were led off down a dark, echoing passage and the armoured creatures once again turned to regard me.

One of them stretched, then lifted off his ornate helm to reveal a white, human face with pale, cold eyes—weary eyes, it seemed to me. He began to unbuckle the straps of his armour and it was drawn away to show the thick padding beneath. When the padding was pulled off, I saw that the body, also, was of perfectly normal proportions. The others stripped off their armour and handed it to those waiting to receive it. As a gesture, I took off my own helmet and held it crooked in my left arm.

The men were all pale, all with the same strange eyes which were not so much unfriendly as introspective. They wore loose tabards which had every inch covered in dark-hued embroidery, trousers of similar material which were baggy and tucked into boots of painted leather.

'Well,' sighed the man who had first removed his armour, 'here we are in Haradeik.' He signed to a servant. 'Seek our master. Tell him Morgeg is here with his patrol. Tell him we have brought a visitor—Urlik Skarsol of the Frozen Keep. Ask him if he would grant us an audience.'

I frowned at Morgeg. 'So you know of Urlik Skarsol. You know that I hail from the Frozen Keep.'

A tiny, puzzled smile came to Morgeg's mouth. 'All know of Urlik Skarsol. But I have heard of no man who has ever met him.'

'And you called this city Rowernarc when we arrived, but now you call it Haradeik.'

'Rowernarc is the city. Haradeik is the name of our particular warren—the province of our master, Bishop Belphig.'

'And who is this bishop?'

'Why, he is one of our two rulers. He is Lord Spiritual of Rowernarc.'

Morgeg spoke in a low, sad tone which I guessed was habitual rather than reflecting a particular mood of his at this moment. Everything he said sounded off-handed. Nothing seemed to matter to him. Nothing seemed to interest him. He seemed almost as dead as the murky, twilight world outside the cavern city.

Quite soon the messenger returned.

'Bishop Belphig grants an audience,' he told Morgeg.

By this time the others had gone about their business and only Morgeg and I remained in the antechamber. Morgeg led me along a poorly lit passage, every inch of which was decorated—even the floor was of crystalline mosaic, and harpies, chimerae and musimonii glared down at me from the low ceiling. Another antechamber, another great door, slightly smaller than the outer one, which withdrew to allow us entrance. And we were in a large hall.

It was a hall with a high arched ceiling coming almost to a point at the top. At the end of it was a dais hung with draperies. On each side of the dais was a glowing brazier, tended by servants, which issued ruddy light and sent smoke curling towards the ceiling where, presumably, it found egress, for there was only a hint of smoke in the air I breathed. As if preserved in volcanic glass, stone monsters writhed and crouched on walls and ceiling, leering, baring unlikely fangs, laughing at some obscene joke, roaring, threatening, twisting in some secret agony. Many bore resemblances to the heraldic monsters of John

33

Daker's world. Here were cockfish, opinicus, mantigoras, satyrs, man-lions, melusines, camelopards, wyverns, cockatrices, dragons, griffins, unicorns, amphisboenae, enfields, bagwyns, salamanders—every combination of man, beast, fish and fowl—all of huge size, rending each other, crawling over each other's backs, copulating, tangling tails, defecating, dying, being born . . .

This, surely, was a chamber of Hell.

I looked towards the dais. Behind draperies, in some sort of throne, a figure lounged. I approached the dais, half expecting the figure to be possessed of a spiked tail and a pair of horns.

A foot or two from the dais Morgeg stopped and bowed. I did likewise. The drapes were drawn back by servants and there sat a man very different from what I had expected—very different from the pale, sad-eyed Morgeg.

The voice was deep, sensuous, jovial. 'Greetings, Count Urlik. We are honoured you should decide to pay a visit to this rat's nest we call Rowernarc, you who are of the free and open icelands.'

Bishop Belphig was fat, dressed in rich robes, a circlet around his long, blond hair, keeping it from his eyes. His lips were very red and his eyebrows very black. With a sudden shock I realised that he was using cosmetics. Beneath them doubtless he, too, was as pale as Morgeg and the rest. Perhaps the hair was dyed. Certainly the cheeks were rouged, the eyelashes false, the lips painted.

'Greetings, Bishop Belphig,' I replied. 'I thank the Lord Spiritual of Rowernarc for his hospitality and would beg a word or two with him in private.'

'Aha! You have some message for me, dear count! Of course. Morgeg—the rest of you—leave us for a while. But stay within earshot if I should want to call you suddenly.'

I smiled slightly. Bishop Belphig did not want to risk the fact that I might be an assassin.

When they had gone Belphig waved a beringed hand in an expansive gesture. 'Well, good count? What is your message?'

'I have no message,' I said. 'I have only a question. Perhaps several questions.'

'Then ask them, sir! Please, ask them!'

'First, I would know why my name is familiar to you all. Secondly, I would ask if it was you, who must have certain mystical knowledge, who summoned me here. The other questions depend on your answers to the first two.'

34

'Why, dear count, your name is known to all! You are a legend, you are a fabulous hero. You must know this!'

'Presume that I have awakened just recently from a deep sleep. Presume that most of my memories are gone. Tell me of the legend.'

Bishop Belphig frowned and he put fat, jewelled fingers to fat, carmine lips. His voice was more subdued, more contemplative when next he spoke. 'Very well, I will presume that. There are said to have been four Ice Lords—of North, South, East and West—but all died save the Lord of the South Ice, who was frozen in his great keep by a sorceress until he should be called for—summoned when his people were in great danger. All this took place in antiquity, only a century or two after the ice had destroyed the famous cities of the world—Barbart, Lanjis Liho, Korodune and the rest.'

The names were faintly familiar but no memories were awakened within me by the remainder of the bishop's story.

'Is there any more of the legend?' I asked.

'That is the substance of it. I can probably find a book or two containing some sort of amplification.'

'And it was not you who called me?'

'Why should I summon you? To tell you the truth, Count Urlik, I did not believe the legend.'

'And you believe it now? You do not think me an impostor?'

'Why should you be an impostor? And if you are, why should I not humour you if it suits you to say you are Count Urlik.' He smiled. 'There is precious little that is new in Rowernarc. We welcome diversion.'

I returned his smile. 'A pleasantly sophisticated view, Bishop Belphig. However, I remain puzzled. Not long since, I found myself on the ice, travelling here. My accoutrements and my name were familiar, but all else was strange. I am a creature, my lord, with little volition of his own. I am a hero, you see, and am called whenever I am needed. I will not bore you with the details of my tragedy, save to say that I would not be here unless I was needed to take part in a struggle. If you did not call me, then perhaps you know who did.'

Belphig drew his painted brows together in a frown. Then he raised them and gave me a quizzical look. 'I fear I can offer no suggestion at present, Count Urlik. The only threat facing Rowernarc is the inevitable one. In a century or two the ice will creep over our mountain barrier and extinguish us. In the meantime, we while away the hours as best we can. You are welcome to join us here, if the Lord Temporal agrees, and you must promise to recount your whole story to us, no matter how incredible you think it is. In return, we can offer you such entertainments as we have. These may be stimulating if they are new to you.'

'Has Rowernarc, then, no enemies?'

'None powerful enough to form a threat. There are a few bands of outlaws, some pirates—the kind of garbage that collects around any city—but they are all.'

I shook my head in puzzlement. 'Perhaps there are internal factions at Rowernarc—groups who wish, say, to overthrow you and the Lord Temporal?'

Bishop Belphig laughed. 'Really, my dear count, you seem to desire strife above all else! I assure you that there are no issues in Rowernarc on which anyone would care to spend much time. Boredom is our only enemy and now that you are here that enemy has been put to flight!'

'Then I thank you for your offer of hospitality,' I said. 'I will accept it. Presumably you have libraries in Rowernarc—and scholars.'

'We are all scholars in Rowernarc. Yes, we have libraries, many of which you may use.'

At least, I thought, I would be able here to spend the best part of my time seeking to find a means of returning to Ermizhad and the lovely world of the Eldren (to which this world was in hateful contrast). Yet I could not believe that I had been called here for nothing, unless it was to a life of exile in which, as an immortal, I would be forced to witness the eventual death of the Earth.

'However,' continued Bishop Belphig, 'I cannot alone make this decision. We must also consult my fellow-ruler, the Lord Temporal. I am sure he will agree to your requests and make you welcome. Apartments must be found for you, and slaves and the like. These activities will also help relieve the ennui which besets Rowernarc.'

'I desire no slaves,' I said.

Bishop Belphig chuckled. 'Wait until you see them before you make your decision.' Then he paused and gave me an amused look from his made-up eyes. 'But perhaps you are of a period where the holding of slaves is frowned upon, eh? I have read that history has had such periods. But in Rowernarc slaves are not held by force. Only those who wish to be slaves are such. If they choose to be something else, why, then, they can be whatever they desire. This is Rowernarc, Count Urlik, where all men and women are free to follow any inclination they choose.'

'And you chose to be Lord Spiritual here?'

Again the bishop smiled. 'In a sense. The title is an hereditary one, but many born to this rank have preferred other occupations. My brother, for instance, is a common sailor.'

'You sail those salt-thick seas?' I was astonished.

'Again—in a sense. If you know not the customs of Rowernarc, I believe you will find many of them interesting.'

'I am sure I will,' I said. And I thought privately that some of those customs I should not find to my taste at all. Here, I thought, I had found the human race in its final stages of decadence—perverse, insouciant, without ambition. And I could not blame them. After all, they had no future.

And there was something, too, in me which reflected Bishop Belphig's cynicism. For had not I little to live for, also?

The bishop raised his voice. 'Slaves! Morgeg! You may return.'

They trooped back into the murky chamber, Morgeg at their head.

'Morgeg,' said the bishop, 'perhaps you will send a messenger to find the Lord Temporal. Ask him if he will grant an audience to Count Urlik Skarsol. Tell him I have offered the count our hospitality, if he should agree.'

Morgeg bowed and left the chamber.

'And now, while we wait, you must dine with me, my lord,' Bishop Belphig said to me. 'We grow fruits and vegetables in our garden caverns and the sea provides us with meat. My cook is the best in all Rowernarc. Will you eat?'

'Gladly,' I said, for I had realised that I was famished.

CHAPTER FOUR

THE LORD TEMPORAL

The meal, though somewhat rich and overspiced for my taste, was delicious. When it was over, Morgeg came back to say that the Lord Temporal had been given the message.

'It was some time before we could find him,' Morgeg said, offering Belphig a significant look. 'But he will give an audience to our guest now, if our guest desires.' He looked at me with his pale, cold eyes.

'Have you had enough to eat and drink, Count Urlik?'
Bishop Belphig asked. 'Is there anything else you desire?' He
wiped his red lips with a brocade napkin, removed a sauce stain
from his jowl.

'I thank you for your generosity,' I said rising. I had drunk
more salty wine than I should have liked, but it helped dampen
the morbid thoughts of Ermizhad which still plagued me—
would plague me for ever, until I found her again.

I followed Morgeg from the grotesque chamber. As I reached
the door I looked back, thinking to thank Bishop Belphig again.

He had smeared some of the sauce over the body of a young
boy slave. As I watched, he bent to lick at the stuff he had put
there.

I turned quickly and increased my stride as Morgeg led me
back the way we had come.

'The Lord Temporal's province is called Dhötgard and lies
above this one. We must go to the outer causeway again.'

'Are there no passages connecting the various levels?' I asked.

Morgeg shrugged. 'Aye, I believe so. But this way is easier
than searching for the doors and then trying to get them open.'

'You mean you do not use many of the passages?'

Morgeg nodded. 'There are fewer of us now than there were
even fifty years ago. Children are rare in Rowernarc these days.'
He spoke carelessly and once again I had the impression that I
spoke to a corpse brought back from the dead.

Through the great main door of Haradeik we passed and into
the cold air of the causeway that hung above the dark bay
where the sluggish sea spread pale salt on the black crystals of
the beach. It seemed an even gloomier landscape than it had
seemed before, with the clouds bringing the horizon so close and
the jagged crags on all other sides. I felt a sense of claustro-
phobia as we walked up the causeway until we came to an
archway which was little different in style from the one we had
just left.

Morgeg cupped his hands together and shouted through
them. 'Lord Urlik Skarsol comes to seek audience with the Lord
Temporal!'

His voice found a muffled echo in the mountains. I looked
up, trying to see the sky, trying to make out the sun behind the
clouds, but I could not.

There was a grating noise as the door slid in just sufficiently for us to squeeze past and find ourselves in an antechamber with smooth walls and even less light than that which had barely illuminated Haradeik. A servant in a plain white tabard was waiting for us. He rang a silver handbell and the door moved back. The machinery operating these doors must have been very sophisticated, for I could see no evidence of pulleys and chains.

The passage we moved down was the twin to the one in Bishop Belphig's 'province' save that here there were no bas-reliefs. Instead there were paintings, but the light was so poor and the paint so old that I could scarcely make out any details. We turned into a similar passage, our footsteps sounding loudly on the carpet-covered floor. Another passage and then we reached an archway which was not blocked by a door. Instead, a curtain of plain, soft leather had been hung across it. I felt that such simplicity was incongruous in Rowernarc, but I was even more surprised when the servant parted the curtain and led us into a chamber whose walls were completely bare, save that they had been covered with a surface of white paint. Huge lamps brightly lit the room. These lamps were probably oil-burning, for a faint smell issued from them. In the middle of the room was a desk and two benches. Save for ourselves, there were no other occupants.

Morgeg looked around at the room and his expression was one of discomfort.

'I will leave you here, Count Urlik. Doubtless the Lord Temporal will emerge soon.'

When Morgeg had left, the servant indicated that I sit on one of the benches. I did so, placing my helm beside me. Like the room, the desk was bare, apart from two scrolls placed neatly near the end. There was nothing for me to do but look at the white walls, the silent servant who had taken up a position by the arch curtain, the almost bare desk.

I must have sat there for an hour before the curtain parted and a tall figure entered. I rose to my feet, hardly able to restrain the expression of astonishment which tried to come over my face. The figure signed for me to sit down again. He had an abstracted look as he walked to the desk and sat behind it.

'I am Shanosfane,' he said.

His skin was a flat, coal black and his features were fine-boned and ascetic. I reflected, ironically, that somehow the roles of Shanosfane and Belphig had become muddled—that Belphig should have been the Temporal Lord and Shanosfane the Spiritual Lord.

Shanosfane wore loose, white robes. The only decoration was a fibula at his left shoulder which bore a device I took to be the sign of his rank. He rested his long-fingered hands on the desk and regarded me with a distant expression which none the less betrayed a great intelligence.

'I am Urlik,' I replied, thinking it best to speak as simply.

He nodded, peering at the desk and tracing a triangle upon it with his finger. 'Belphig said you wished to stay here.' His voice was deep, resonant, far away.

'He told me there were books I might consult.'

'There are many books here, though most are of a whimsical kind. The pursuit of true knowledge no longer interests the folk of Rowernarc, Lord Urlik. Did Bishop Belphig tell you that?'

'He merely said I should find books here. Also he told me that all men were scholars in Rowernarc.'

A gleam of irony came into Shanosfane's dark eyes. 'Scholars? Aye. Scholars in the art of the perverse.'

'You seem to disapprove of your own people, my lord.'

'How can I disapprove of the damned, Count Urlik? And we are all damned—they and I. It has been our misfortune to be born at the end of Time . . .'

I spoke feelingly. 'It is no misfortune if death is all you have to face.'

With curiosity he looked up. 'You do not fear death, then?'

I shrugged. 'I do not know death. I am immortal.'

'Then you are really from the Frozen Keep?'

'I do not know my origins. I have been many heroes. I have seen many ages of the Earth.'

'Indeed?' His interest grew and I could tell it was a purely intellectual interest. There was no empathy here, save possibly of minds. There was no emotion. 'Then you are a traveller in Time?'

'I am, in a sense, though not, I think, the sense you mean.'

'Some several centuries—or perhaps millenia—ago there was a race of folk lived on the Earth. I heard they learnt the art of time-travel and left this world, for they knew it was dying. But doubtless it is a legend. But then, so are you a legend, Count Urlik. And you exist.'

'You believe that I am no impostor, then?'

'I think that is what I believe. In what sense do you travel in Time?'

'I am drawn wherever I am called. Past, present and future have no meaning for me. Ideas of cyclical time have little meaning, for I believe there are many universes, many alternative destinies. The history of this planet might never have included me, in any of my incarnations. And yet it might have included them all.'

'Strange...' Shanosfane spoke musingly, raising a delicate black hand to his fine brow. 'For our universe is so confined and clearly marked, while yours is vast, chaotic. If—forgive me— you are not insane, then some theories of mine are confirmed. Interesting...'

'It is my intention,' I continued, 'to seek the means of returning to one of these worlds, if it still exists, and using everything in my power to remain there.'

'It does not excite you to move from world to world, from Time to Time?'

'Not for eternity, Lord Shanosfane. Not when, on one of those worlds, is a being for whom I have an abiding love and who shares that love.'

'How found you that world?'

I began to speak. Soon I discovered that I was telling him my whole story, everything that had happened to me since John Daker had been called by King Rigenos to aid the forces of humanity against the Eldren, every fragment of my recollections of other incarnations, everything that had befallen me until the Rowernarc patrol had met me on the beach. He listened with great attention, staring up at the ceiling as I spoke, never interrupting me, until I had finished.

He said nothing for a while, but then signed to his patient servant. 'Bring water and some rice.' For a few moments more he considered my story. I thought he must surely believe me a madman now.

'You say you were called to come here,' he said eventually. 'Yet we did not call you. It is unlikely that, whatever the danger, we should place much faith in a legend of the sort that has existed throughout history if my reading is accurate on the matter.'

'Are there any others who might have summoned me?'

'Yes.'

'Bishop Belphig said this was unlikely.'

'Belphig shapes his thoughts to fit his moods. There are communities beyond Rowernarc, there are cities beyond the sea. At least, there were, before the Silver Warriors came.'

'Belphig mentioned nothing of the Silver Warriors.'

'Perhaps he forgot. It has been some while since we last heard

41

of them.'

'Who are they?'

'Oh, ravagers of some description. Their motives are obscure.'

'Where do they come from?'

'They come from Moon, I think.'

'From the sky? Where is Moon?'

'On the other side of the world, they say. The few references I have seen do mention that it was once in the sky, but no longer.'

'These Silver Warriors—are they human.'

'Not according to the accounts I received.'

'And do they offer you harm, Lord Shanosfane? Will they try to invade Rowernarc?'

'Perhaps. I think they want the planet for themselves.'

I looked at him feeling somewhat shocked by his lack of interest.

'You do not care if they destroy you?'

'Let them have the planet. What use is it to us? Our race will soon be overwhelmed by the ice that creeps a little closer each year as the sun fades. These people seem better adapted to live in the world than we are.'

Though I could understand his argument, I had never encountered such complete disinterest before. I admired it, but I felt little true sympathy with it. It was my destiny to struggle—though for what cause I had no clear idea—and even while I hated the fact that I must do battle through eternity (or so it seemed) my instincts were still those of a warrior.

While I tried to think of an answer, the black Lord Temporal rose. 'Well, we will talk again. You may live in Rowernarc until you desire to leave.'

And with that he left the room.

As he left, the servant entered with the tray of rice and water. He turned and, holding the tray, followed behind his master.

Now that I had met both the Lord Spiritual and the Lord Temporal of Rowernarc I was even more confused than when I had first arrived here. Why had Belphig not told me of the alien Silver Warriors? Was I destined to fight them or—another thought came—were the folk of Rowernarc the enemy I had been called to war against?

CHAPTER FIVE

THE BLACK SWORD

And so, unhappy, torn by my longing for Ermizhad, by my great sense of loss, I settled in the Obsidian City of Rowernarc, there to brood, to pore over ancient books in strange scripts, to seek some solution to my tragic dilemma and yet feel my despair increasing with every day that passed.

To be accurate, there were no days and nights in the Obsidian City. People slept, awakened and ate when they felt like it and their other appetites were followed in the same spirit, for all that those appetites were jaded and novelty did not exist.

I had been given my own apartments on the level below Haradeik, Bishop Belphig's province. Though they were not quite as baroque as the bishop's apartments, I would have preferred the simplicity which Shanosfane's had. I learned, however, that Shanosfane himself had ordered most decoration removed from Dhötgard when he had assumed his position on the death of his father. The apartments were more than comfortable—the most committed sybarite would have found them luxurious—but for the first weeks of my stay I was plagued with visitors.

It was a seducer's dream, but for me, with my love for Ermizhad unwaning, it was a nightmare.

Woman after woman would present herself in my bedchamber, offering me more exotic delights than even Faust had known. As politely as I could—and much to their astonishment—I refused them all. Men, too, came with similar promises and, because the customs of Rowernarc were such that these advances were not considered shameful, I refused them with equal politeness.

And then Bishop Belphig would arrive with presents—young slaves as covered in cosmetics as he was—rich foodstuffs for which I had no appetite—books of erotic verse which did not interest me—suggestions of acts which might be committed upon my person which disgusted me. Since I owed my roof and the possibility of research to Belphig, I retained my patience with him and judged that he only meant well, though I found both his tastes and his appearance sinister.

On my visits to the various libraries situated on different levels of the Obsidian City I witnessed sights which I would not have believed existed outside the pages of Dante's *Inferno*. Orgies were unceasing. I would stumble upon them wherever I went. In some of the libraries I visited I found them. And they were never orgies of plain fornication.

Torture was common and witnessed by whoever chose to be a spectator. That the victims were willing did not make the sights any easier for me to bear. Even murder itself was not outlawed, for the murdered man or woman desired death as much as the murderer desired to kill.

These pale people with no future, no hope, nothing to prepare for save death, spent their days in experimenting with pain quite as much as they experimented with pleasure.

Rowenarc was a city gone mad. A dreadful neurosis had settled upon it and it seemed pitiful to me that these people, so sophisticated and talented, should waste their final years in such ultimately self-destructive pursuits.

The grotesque galleries and halls and passages would ring to the sound of screams—high-pitched screams of laughter, ululating screams of terror—with moans, with grunts and bellowings.

Through all this I would stride, sometimes tripping over a prone, drugged body in the gloom, sometimes having to disentangle myself from the arms of a naked girl barely out of puberty.

Even the books I found were frustrating. Lord Shanosfane had warned me in his own way. Most of the books were examples of completely decadent prose, so convoluted as to be nearly meaningless. Not only works of fiction, but all the works of fact, were written in this manner. My brain would spin as I attempted to make sense of it all—and failed.

At other times, when I had given up trying to interpret these decadent texts, I would pass through a gallery and see Lord Shanosfane wandering across a hall, his ascetic face frozen in abstracted thought, while all around him his subjects sported, sometimes leering and gesturing at him obscenely. Occasionally he would look up, put his head to one side, regard them with a slight frown and then walk on.

The first few times I saw him I hailed him, but he ignored me as he would have ignored anyone else. I wondered what ideas were forming and re-forming in that strange, cool brain. I felt sure that if he would grant me another audience I would learn much more from him than I had managed to learn from the texts I studied, but since the first day I had arrived at Rowernarc he had not agreed to see me.

My sojourn in Rowernarc was so much like a dream itself that perhaps that was the reason why my slumber was dreamless for the first fifty nights of my stay there. But on what I reckon to be the fifty-first night, those familiar visions returned.

They had terrified me as I lay in Ermizhad's arms. Now I almost welcomed them...

I stood on a hill and spoke with a faceless knight in black and yellow armour. A pale flag without insignia fluttered on a staff erected between us.

Below us, in the valley, towns and cities were burning. Red fires sprouted everywhere. Black smoke cruised above the scenes of carnage from time to time revealed.

It seemed to me that the whole human race fought in that valley—every human being who had ever drawn breath was there, save me.

I saw great armies marching back and forth. I saw ravens and vultures feasting on battlefields. I heard the distant sounds of drums and guns and trumpets.

'You are Count Urlik Skarsol of the Frozen Keep,' said the faceless knight.

'I am Erekosë, adopted Prince of the Eldren,' I replied firmly.

The faceless knight laughed. 'No longer, warrior. No longer.'

'Why am I made to suffer so, Sir Knight in Black and Yellow?'

'You need not suffer—not if you accepted your fate. After all, you cannot die. True you may seem to perish, but your incarnations are infinite.'

'But that knowledge is what causes the suffering! If I could not remember previous incarnations, then I would believe each life to be my only one.'

'Some people would give much for such knowledge.'

'The knowledge is only partial. I know my fate, but I do not know how I earned it. I do not understand the structure of the universe through which I am flung, seemingly at random.'

'It is a random universe. It has no permanent structure.'

'At least you have told me that.'

'I will answer any question you put to me. Why should I lie?'

'Then that is my first question: Why should you lie?'

'You are over-cunning, Sir Champion. I should lie if I wished to deceive you.'

'Do you lie?'

'The answer is ...'

The knight in black and yellow faded. The armies were marching around and around the hills, up and down them, in all directions across the valley. They were singing many different songs, but one song reached my ears.

> 'All Empires fall,
> All ages die,
> All strife shall be in vain.
> All kings go down,
> All hope must fail,
> But Tanelorn remains—
>   Our Tanelorn remains ...'

A simple soldier's chant, but it meant something to me— something important. Had I once belonged to this place Tanelorn? Or had I sought to find it?

I could not distinguish which of the armies was singing the song. But it was already fading away.

> 'All words must die,
> Fade into night,
> But Tanelorn remains—
>   Our Tanelorn remains ...'

Tanelorn.

The sense of loss I had felt when parted from Ermizhad came to me then—and I associated it with Tanelorn.

It seemed to me that if I could find Tanelorn, I would find the key to my destiny, find a means of ending my misery and my doom ...

Now another figure stood on the other side of the plain flag and still the armies marched below us, still the towns and cities burned.

I looked at the figure.

'Ermizhad!'

Ermizhad smiled sadly. 'I am not Ermizhad! Just as you have one spirit and many forms, so has Ermizhad one form but many spirits!'

'There is only one Ermizhad!'

'Aye—but many who resemble her.'

'Who are you?'

'I am myself.'

I turned away. I knew that she spoke truth and was not Ermizhad, but I could not bear to look on Ermizhad's face; I was tired of riddles.

Then I said to her: 'Do you know of Tanelorn?'

'Many know of Tanelorn. Many have sought her. She is an old city. She has lasted through eternity.'

'How may I reach Tanelorn?'

'Only you may answer that question, Champion.'

'Where lies Tanelorn? On Urlik's world?'

'Tanelorn exists in many Realms, on many Planes, in many Worlds, for Tanelorn is eternal. Sometimes hidden, sometimes there for all to visit—though most do not realise the nature of the city—Tanelorn shelters many Heroes.'

'Will I find Ermizhad if I find Tanelorn?'

'You will find what you truly desire to find. But first you must take up the Black Sword again.'

'Again? Have I borne a black sword before?

'Many times.'

'And where shall I find the sword?'

'You will know it. You will always know the Black Sword for to bear it is your destiny and your tragedy.'

And then she, too, was gone.

But the armies continued to march and the valley continued to burn and over my head the standard without insignia still flew.

Then, where she had been, something inhuman materialised, turned into a smoky substance, formed itself into a different shape.

And I did recognise that shape. It was the Black Sword. A huge, black broadsword carved with runes of terrifying import.

I backed away.

'NO! I WILL NEVER AGAIN WIELD THE BLACK SWORD!'

And a sardonic voice, full of evil and wisdom, seemed to issue from the blade itself.

'THEN YE SHALL NEVER KNOW PEACE!'

'BEGONE!'

'I AM THINE—ONLY THINE. THOU ART THE ONLY MORTAL WHO CAN BEAR ME!'

'I REFUSE YOU!'

'THEN CONTINUE TO SUFFER!'

I awoke shouting. I was sweating. My throat and mouth were parched.

The Black Sword. I knew the name now. I knew that it was somehow tied up with my destiny.

But the rest—had it been merely a nightmare Or had it offered me information in a symbolic form? I had no means of telling.

In the darkness I flung out an arm and touched warm flesh. I was back with Ermizhad again!

I took that naked body to me. I bent to kiss the lips.

Lips raised themselves to mine. Lascivious lips that were hot and coarse. The body writhed against me. A woman began to whisper obscenities into my ear.

I leapt back with an oath. Rage and disappointment consumed me. It was not Ermizhad. It was one of the women of Rowernarc who had slipped into my bed while I lay experiencing my dreadful dreams.

Despair swept through me, wave upon wave. I sobbed. The woman laughed.

And then something filled me—some emotion that seemed alien to me and yet which possessed me.

Fiercely I flung myself on the girl.

'Very well,' I promised, 'if you will have such pleasures—then have them all!'

And in the morning I lay in my disordered bed exhausted while the woman clambered from it and staggered away, a strange expression upon her features. I do not think pleasures were what she had experienced. I know that I had not. I felt only disgusted with myself for what I had done.

All the while one image remained in my brain. It was to rid myself of that image, I think, that I had taken the girl as I had. Perhaps the image had driven me to do what I had done. I do not know. I did know, however, that I would do it again if it would burn the image of the Black Sword from my mind for only a few moments.

There were no dreams the next night, but the old fear had returned. And when the girl I had ravaged the night before came to my room simpering I almost dismissed her before I learned that she came with a message from Bishop Belphig whose slave she apparently was.

'My master says that a change of scenery might improve your temper. Tomorrow he embarks on a great Sea Hunt and asks if you would care to join him.'

I flung down the book I was trying to interpret. 'Aye,' I said. 'I'll come. It sounds a healthier way of wasting time than puzzling over these damned books.'

'Will you take me with you, Lord Urlik?'

The heated expression on her face, the moist lips, the way she held herself, all made me shudder.

But I shrugged my shoulders.

'Why not?'

She chuckled. 'And shall I bring a tasty friend?'

'Do what you wish.'

But when she had gone I flung myself down to my knees on that hard, obsidian floor and I buried my head in my arms and I wept.

'Ermizhad! Oh, Ermizhad!'

CHAPTER SIX

THE GREAT SALT SEA

I joined Bishop Belphig on the outer causeway the next morning. Even in the light of that perpetual dusk I could see better the face the cosmetics sought to hide. There were the jowls, the pouched eyes, the down-curved, self-indulgent mouth, the lines of depravity, all smeared about with colours and creams, serving only to make his appearance that much more hideous.

The Lord Spiritual's entourage was with him—painted boys and girls giggling and simpering, carrying pieces of luggage, shivering in the dull coldness of the outer air.

The bishop put a fat arm through one of mine and led me ahead of the crowd, down towards the bay where the strange ship waited.

I suffered this gesture and looked back to see if my weapons were being brought. They were. Slaves staggered along with my long, silver-shod spear and battle-axe. Why I had decided to bring these weapons I do not know, but the bishop plainly did not think my decision incongruous though I was not at all sure he was pleased about it, either.

For all its decadence and despair, I did not find Rowernarc itself menacing. The people offered me no harm and, once aware that I did not wish to join in their sports, tended for the most part to leave me to my own devices. They were neutral. Lord Shanosfane, too, had an air of neutrality. But I did not get this impression of Bishop Belphig. There was, indeed, something sinister about him and I was beginning to feel that he was perhaps the sole member of that peculiar community who possessed some sort of motive, however perverse; some ambition beyond the need to find new ways of whiling away the days.

Yet for all appearances Bishop Belphig was the most dedicated of all sybarites and it was my possibly puritanical eye that saw menace in him. I reminded myself that he was the sole inhabitant of Rowernarc who had displayed any sort of deviousness.

'Well, my dear Lord Urlik, what do you think of our craft?' Belphig gestured towards the ship with a fat, beringed finger. He was dressed in the bulbous armour I had originally seen worn by the riders on the beach, but his helm was being carried by a slave. A brocade cloak flowed from his shoulders.

'I have never seen an odder craft,' I replied frankly.

We were approaching the shore and I could see the craft quite clearly. She was quite close to the beach on which stood a number of figures whom I guessed were part of her crew. She was about forty feet in length and about ten feet high. As ornately decorated as anything else of Rowernarc, plated with reliefs of silver, bronze and gold, she had a kind of pyramidal superstructure on which were situated various terraces—a succession of narrow decks. At the top was a square deck from which several banners flew. The hull was raised above the level of the ocean on struts connected to a broad, flat, slightly curved sheet of highly polished material resembling something very like fibreglass and resting on the water. She had no masts but on each side were arranged wheels of broad-bladed paddles. Unlike the blades of a paddle-steamer, these were not contained within an outer wheel but were naked. But even the large paddles did not seem strong enough to push the craft through the water.

'You must have very powerful engines,' I commented.

'Engines?' Belphig chuckled. 'She has no engines.'

'Then . . . ?'

'Wait until we are aboard.'

The group of people waiting on the beach had two litters ready. Plainly these were meant for us. Belphig and I crunched across the crystal until we reached them. Then the bishop entered one and, somewhat reluctantly, I climbed into the other. The alternative, I guessed, was to wade through that murky, viscous water and merely the sight of it filled me with distaste. A grey scum floated at the edges where it touched the beach and the smell of decay and ordure reached my nostrils. I guessed that this was the place into which Rowernarc's waste found its way.

The litters were lifted up and the slaves began to wade through the water that appeared to have the consistency of porridge and which had oily black weed growing on its surface.

A flight of collapsible steps had been lowered down the side of the ship and Belphig led the way up them, puffing and complaining until we were aboard and entering a doorway at the base of the pyramid.

Up we went again until we at last reached the top deck and stood on it, watching the rest of the crew and entourage assembling themselves on the various lower galleries. The prow of the ship was raised and curved and had a high gallery of its own which was protected by a rail of rococo iron. From this gallery what appeared to be long ropes went over the side and into the water. They were secured to stanchions and I took them to be anchor ropes.

Looking over the ship I had the peculiar impression that we were aboard a gigantic cart rather than a sea-going vessel, for the paddle-wheels were arranged on spokes, in pairs, with nothing, apparently, to drive them.

The slave arrived with my spear and axe and handed them to me. I thanked him and fixed them into lugs which were arranged for this purpose around the inside of the rail.

Belphig looked up at the sky, as an ordinary sailor might look to see the lie of the weather. I could see no change in the thick, brown cloud layers, the jagged mountain peaks or the sluggish sea. The sun was again invisible and its faint light was further diffused by the clouds. I drew my heavy coat about me and waited impatiently for Bishop Belphig to give the order to sail.

I was already regretting my decision to accompany the Lord Spiritual on this venture. I had no idea what we were to hunt or in what manner. My sense of discomfort was increasing as some instinct warned me that the bishop had invited me on this hunt for more specific reasons than the relief of my boredom.

Morgeg, the bishop's captain, climbed the central stairway to the top deck and presented himself to his master.

'We are ready to roll, Lord Bishop.'

'Good.' Belphig put a pale hand on my arm in a confiding gesture. 'Now you will see our "engines", Count Urlik.' He smiled secretly at Morgeg. 'Give the order, Sir Morgeg.'

Morgeg leaned over the rail and addressed the armoured men who had now taken up positions in the prow gallery. They were strapped into seats and had the ropes that I thought anchor ropes around their arms. There were whips in their hands, long harpoons at their sides. 'Prepare!' shouted Morgeg through cupped hands. The armoured men stiffened and drew back the arms holding the whips. 'Begin!'

As one, the whips snapped out and cracked the surface of the water. Three times they did this and then I saw a disturbance just ahead of the prow and gasped as something began to emerge from below.

Then four huge, gnarled heads broke from the depths. The heads turned to glare at the whipmen in the prow. Strange, barking noises came from the sinuous throats. Monstrous, serpentine bodies threshed in the water. The beasts had flat heads from the mouths of which long, straight tusks protruded. A harness was attached to these heads and with tugs the whipmen forced them to turn until they were looking out to sea.

Again the whips cracked and the beasts began to move.

With a lurch the ship was off, its paddles not cutting *through* the water but supporting the ship *on* the water, as wheels support a chariot.

And that was what the ship was—a huge chariot designed to roll over the surface, pulled by these ugly monsters that seemed to me to be a cross between sea-serpents of legend, sea-lions of John Daker's world, with a trace of sabre-tooth tiger for good measure!

Out into that nightmare ocean swam the nightmare beasts, pulling our impossible craft behind them.

The whips cracked louder and the drivers sang out to the beasts who swam faster. The wheels rolled rapidly and soon Rowernarc's terrible shore disappeared in murky brown cloud.

We were alone on that nameless, hellish sea.

Bishop Belphig had become animated. He had placed his helm on his head and had opened the visor. In its nest of steel his face looked even more depraved.

'Well, Count Urlik. What do you think of our engines?'

'I have never seen such beasts. I could never have imagined them. How do you manage to train them?'

'Oh, they were bred for this work—they are domestic animals. Once Rowernarc had many scientists. They built our city, channelling our heat from the fires that still flickered in the bowels of the planet. They designed and built our ships. They bred our various beasts of burden. But that, of course, was a thousand years ago. We have no need of such scientists now ...'

I thought it a slightly odd statement, though I said nothing. Instead, I asked: 'And what do we hunt, my lord bishop?'

Belphig drew a deep, excited breath. 'Nothing less than the sea-stag himself. It is dangerous work. We might all perish.'

'The thought of dying in this dreadful ocean does not commend itself,' I said.

He chuckled. 'Aye, a foul death. Perhaps the worst death this world can offer. But that is where the thrill lies, does it not?'

'For you, perhaps.'

'Ah, come now, Count Urlik. I thought you were beginning to enjoy our ways.'

'You know that I am grateful for your hospitality. Without it I suppose I would have perished. But "enjoy" is not the word I would have chosen.'

He licked his lips, his pale eyes bright and lascivious. 'But the slave girl I sent ...?'

I drew a heavy breath of that cold, salt-clogged air. 'I had had a nightmare shortly before I discovered her in my bed. It seemed to me that she was merely part of that nightmare.'

Belphig laughed and clapped me on the back. 'Oho, you lusty dog! No need to be shy in Rowernarc. The girl told me all!'

I turned away and put my two hands on the rail, staring over the dark waters. A rime of salt had formed on my face and beard, scouring my flesh. I welcomed it.

The sea-beasts strained and threshed and barked, the wheels of the ship slapped the surface of the salt-thick water, Bishop Belphig chuckled and exchanged glances with the dead-faced Morgeg. Sometimes the brown clouds broke and I saw the contracted sphere of the dull, red sun like a jewel hanging from a cavern roof. Sometimes the clouds gathered so close that they blotted out all the light and we moved through pitch darkness broken only by the faint illumination of our artificial torches. A faint wind came and ruffled my coat, stirred the limp banners on their masts, but scarcely brought a ripple to the viscous ocean.

Within me my torment seethed. My lips formed the syllables of Ermizhad's name but then refused to move as if to utter that name, even under my breath, was to taint it.

Onward the ship rolled. Its crew, the slaves of despair, moved about upon its decks or sat listlessly against its rails.

And all the time Bishop Belphig's fat jowls shook as his obscene laughter bubbled through the air.

I began to think that I did not in the least care now if I perished in the waters of that great salt sea.

CHAPTER SEVEN

THE BELL AND THE CHALICE

Later Belphig retired to his cabin with his slaves and the girl who had brought me the message came on deck and put her warm hand on my cold one.

'Master? Do you not want me?'

'Give yourself to Morgeg or whoever else desires you,' I said hollowly, 'and I beg you forget that other time.'

'But, master, you told me I could bring someone else, also ... I thought you had learned to take pleasure in our ways ...'

'I take no pleasure in your ways. Please go.'

She left me alone on the deck. I rubbed at my weary eyes. They were encrusted with salt. After a few moments I, too, went below, sought my cabin, locked the door and ignored the shut-bunk with its profusion of furs and silks in favour of the hammock, doubtless slung there for a servant's use.

Rocked in the hammock, I was soon asleep.

Dreams came, but they were faint dreams. A few scenes. A few words. But the only words that made me shiver were the words which forced me to wake myself:

BLACK SWORD
BLACK SWORD
BLACK SWORD
THE BLACK SWORD IS THE CHAMPION'S SWORD
THE WORD OF THE SWORD IS THE CHAMPION'S LAW
BLACK SWORD
BLACK SWORD
BLACK SWORD
THE BLADE OF THE SWORD HAS THE BLOOD OF THE SUN
THE HILT OF THE SWORD AND THE HAND ARE AS ONE

BLACK SWORD
BLACK SWORD
BLACK SWORD
THE RUNES ON THE SWORD ARE THE WORMS THAT ARE WISE
THE NAME OF THE SWORD IS THE SAME AS THE SCYTHE
BLACK SWORD
BLACK SWORD
BLACK . . .

The rhythm continued to drum in my skull. I shook my head and half fell from my hammock. Outside the cabin I heard hasty footsteps. Now they sounded above my head. I went to a washstand, splashed water over my hands and face, opened the door and climbed the intricately carved companionway to the top deck.

Morgeg and another man stood there. They were leaning over the rail, their ears cocked to the wind. Below, in the prow, the drivers continued to lash the sea-beasts on.

Morgeg stepped back from the rail when he saw me. There was a trace of concern in his pale eyes.

'What is it?' I asked.

He shrugged his shoulders. 'We thought we heard something. A sound we have not heard before in these waters.'

I listened for a while with some concentration but all I could hear was the crack of the drivers' whips, the slap of the wheels on the water.

Then I heard it. A faint booming ahead of us. I peered into the murky brown fog. The booming came more strongly now.

'It's a bell!' I said.

Morgeg frowned.

'A bell! Perhaps there are rocks ahead and they are warning us off.'

Morgeg jerked his thumb at the sea-beasts. 'The *slevahs* would sense rocks if they were near and turn aside.'

The sound of the tolling bell increased. It must have come from a huge bell, for it was deep and the ship vibrated with the noise.

Even the sea-beasts were disturbed by it. They tried to turn away, but the drivers' whips kept them on course.

Still the tolling grew in intensity until it seemed to surround us.

Bishop Belphig appeared on deck. He was not wearing his armour, but some kind of nightshirt by the look of it. Over this he had thrown a huge fur. His cosmetics were smeared and only half applied. Doubtless the bell had disturbed him in the middle of his revels. There was fear on his face.

'Do you know what that bell is?' I asked him.

'No. No.'

But I thought that he did know—or that he guessed what it was. And he was afraid of the bell.

Morgeg said: 'Bladrak's——'

'Silence!' Belphig snapped. 'How could it be?'

'What is Bladrak?' I said.

'Nothing,' Morgeg murmured, his eyes on the bishop.

I did not pursue the subject, but the sense of menace I had felt when first boarding the craft now increased.

The tolling was so loud now that it hurt my ears to hear it.

'Turn the ship about,' Belphig said. 'Give the order, Morgeg. Hurry!'

His evident fear I found almost amusing after the bland impression of self-assurance he had given me earlier.

'Are we going back to Rowernarc?' I asked him.

'Yes, we'll...' He frowned, his eyes flashing first to me, then to Morgeg, then to the rail. He tried to smile. 'No, I think not.'

'Why have you changed your mind?' I asked.

'Be quiet, curse you!' Immediately he controlled himself. 'Forgive me, Count Urlik. This dreadful noise. My nerves...' And he disappeared down the companionway.

Still the bell boomed, but the drivers were turning the *slevahs* now. They reared and threshed in the water, dragging the ship full about.

The drivers lashed them again and their speed increased.

The booming continued, but it was just a little fainter now.

Spray rose with the speed and force with which the wheels slapped the sea's surface. The huge sea-chariot rocked and jolted and I clung hard to the rail.

The tolling of the bell subsided.

Soon silence sat upon the sea once again.

Bishop Belphig re-emerged, clad in his armour, wearing his cloak. His cosmetics had been properly applied, but I saw that the face beneath them was paler than usual. He bowed to me, nodded to Morgeg. He tried to smile.

'I am sorry that I lost my head for a moment, Count Urlik. I had but recently awakened. I was disorientated. That sound was terrifying, was it not?'

'More terrifying, I suspect, to you than to me, Bishop Belphig. I thought you recognised it.'

'No.'

'And so did Morgeg—he uttered a name—Bladrak...'

'A legend of the sea.' Belphig waved his fat hand dismissively. 'Um—concerning a monster, Bladrak, with a voice like a huge bell. Naturally Morgeg, who is of a superstitious turn of mind, thought that Bladrak had come to—er—gobble us up.' His titter was high-pitched, his tone completely unconvincing.

However, as the man's guest I could scarcely push my questioning any farther. I had to accept what was, to me, evidently a hastily invented lie. I returned to my cabin as Belphig instructed Morgeg in a fresh course. And in my cabin I again found the girl I had dismissed. She was lying in the bed, smiling at me, completely naked.

I returned her smile and climbed into my hammock.

But I was soon to be disturbed again.

Almost as soon as I had closed my eyes I heard a shout from above.

Again I leapt from the hammock and rushed up on to the top-deck.

This time I heard no bells, but Morgeg and Belphig were calling down to a sailor on a lower deck. I heard the sailor's voice.

'I swear I saw it! A light to port!'

'We are miles from the nearest land,' Morgeg argued.

'Then perhaps, sir, it was a ship.'

'Is this another legend coming true?' I asked Belphig. He started when he heard me and straightened up.

'I really cannot understand it all, Count Urlik. I think the sailor is imagining things. Once you get one unexplained event at sea, others quickly follow, eh?'

I nodded. There was truth in that. But then I saw a light. I pointed. 'It must be another ship.'

'The light is too bright for a ship.'

I then found an opportunity to put a question to him which had been on my mind since my meeting with Lord Shanosfane. 'What if it is the Silver Warriors?'

Belphig darted me a penetrating look. 'What do you know of the Silver Warriors?'

'Very little. Their race is not the same as yours. They have conquered most of the farther shore of this sea. They are thought to come from a land called Moon on the other side of the world.'

He relaxed. 'And who told you all this?'

'My Lord Shanosfane of Dhötgard—the Lord Temporal.'

'He knows little of the events in the world,' Bishop Belphig said. 'He is more interested in abstracted speculation. The Silver Warriors are not a great threat. They have harried one or two cities of the farther shore, that is true, but I believe they have disappeared again now.'

'Why did you not tell me of them when I asked if you had any enemies or potential enemies?'

'What? Enemies?' Belphig laughed. 'I do not consider warriors from the other side of the world, who have never offered us threat, *enemies*!'

'Not even potential enemies?'

'Not even that. How could they attack us? Rowernarc is impregnable.'

The hoarse voice of the sailor came again. 'There! There it is!'

He was right.

And also I seemed to hear a voice calling over the ocean. A lost voice, an ethereal voice.

'Some mariner in trouble perhaps?' I suggested.

Bishop Belphig assumed an impatient expression. 'Most unlikely.'

Both light and voice were coming closer. I made out a word. It was a very definite word.

'BEWARE!' cried the voice. 'BEWARE!'

Belphig sniffed. 'A pirate's trick, maybe. Best ready the warriors, Morgeg.'

Morgeg went below.

And then the source of the light was much closer and a peculiar screaming began. A wail.

It was a huge golden cup, suspended against the darkness. A great chalice. Both the bright light and the wailing came from it.

Belphig staggered back, shielding his eyes. Doubtless he had never seen such brightness in his whole life.

A voice spoke once again.

'URLIK SKARSOL, IF YOU WOULD RID THIS WORLD OF ITS TROUBLES AND FIND A SOLUTION TO YOUR OWN—YOU MUST TAKE UP THE BLACK SWORD AGAIN.'

The voice of my dreams had entered the realm of reality. Now it was my turn to be terrified.

'No!' I shouted. 'I will never wield the Black Sword. I swore I would not!'

Though I spoke the words, they did not come from my conscious brain, for I still had no idea what the Black Sword was and why I refused to use it. These words were spoken by all the warriors I had been and all the warriors I was to become.

'YOU MUST!'

'I will not!'

'IF YOU DO NOT, THIS WORLD WILL PERISH.'

'It is already doomed!'

'NOT SO!'

'Who are you?' I could not believe that this was a supernatural manifestation. Everything I had experienced so far had had some kind of understandable explanation—but not this screaming chalice—not this voice that boomed from the heavens like the voice of God. I tried to peer at the great golden cup, see what held it, but apparently nothing did hold it.

'Who are you?' I shouted again.

Bishop Belphig's unhealthy face was wreathed in light. It writhed in terror.

'I AM THE VOICE OF THE CHALICE. YOU MUST TAKE UP THE BLACK SWORD.'

'I will not!'

'BECAUSE YOU WOULD NOT LISTEN FROM WITHIN, I HAVE COME TO YOU IN THIS FORM TO IMPRESS UPON YOU THAT YOU MUST TAKE UP THE BLACK SWORD——'

'I will not! I swore I would not!'

'—AND WHEN YOU HAVE TAKEN UP THE SWORD, THEN YOU MAY FILL THE CHALICE! ANOTHER CHANCE WILL NOT COME, ETERNAL CHAMPION.'

I clapped my hands to my ears, closing my eyes tight shut.

I felt the light fade.

I opened my eyes.

The screaming chalice had disappeared. There was only gloom again.

Belphig was shaking with fear. It was plain, when he looked at me, that he associated me with the source of his terror.

I said grimly: 'That was no doing of mine, I assure you.'

Belphig cleared his throat several times before he spoke. 'I have heard of men able to create illusions, Count Urlik, but never illusions so powerful. I am impressed, but I hope you will not see fit to use your power again on this voyage. Merely because I could not answer your questions concerning that bell does not mean that you can——'

'If that were an illusion, Bishop Belphig, it was no creation of mine.'

Belphig began to speak, then changed his mind. Shuddering, he went below.

CHAPTER EIGHT

THE SEA-STAG'S LAIR

I stayed on the deck for a long time, peering into the twilight, wondering if I would see something that would give me a clue as to the origin of that strange visitation. Save for the experience in my bedroom on the Eldren Earth, when I had seen myself as I now was, this was the first time that my dreams had come in waking hours.

And it had been no dream, of course, because Bishop Belphig had witnessed it—as had many members of his crew and entourage. On the lower terraces they were murmuring among themselves, looking up at me in some trepidation, doubtless hoping I would bring no further manifestations of that sort upon them.

But if the screaming chalice had been connected with me, the unseen bell had been connected in some way with Bishop Belphig.

And why was Belphig continuing with the hunt, when any sensible person would have returned to the safety of the Obsidian City? Perhaps he had arranged a rendezvous with someone in these waters? But with whom? One of the pirates he had mentioned? Perhaps even the Silver Warriors?

But these were minor matters of speculation compared with the latest event. What was the Black Sword? Why did something within me refuse it, even though I did not know what it was. Certainly the name had a peculiar sort of familiarity and it was also plain that I did not wish to think about it—that was why I had taken the girl that night. It seemed I was ready to do anything to forget the sword, to escape from it.

At length, weary and full of confusion, I returned to my quarters and fell into my hammock.

But I could not sleep. I did not want to sleep, for fear the dreams would return.

I remembered the words: *If you would rid this world of its troubles and find a solution to your own, you must take up the Black Sword again.*

And the monotonous chant came back to be: *Black Sword. Black Sword. Black Sword. The Black Sword is the Champion's sword—the Word of the Sword is the Champion's Law* ...

In some previous incarnation—whether in the past or the future, for Time in my own context was a meaningless word—I must have rid myself of the Black Sword. And in parting with it I had, say, committed a crime (or at least had offended someone or something which desired that I retain the sword) for which I was now being punished by being moved hither and yon through Time and Space. Or perhaps, as my dream had suggested, the punishment was that I be *aware* of my incarnations and thus know my true tragedy. A subtle punishment if that were so.

Although I desired nothing more than rest and a chance to be reunited with Ermizhad, something in me still refused to pay the price which was my agreement that I would take up the Black Sword again.

The Blade of the Sword has the Blood of the Sun—The Hilt of the Sword and the Hand are as One ...

A rather more cryptic statement. I had no idea what the first part meant. Presumably the second part simply meant that my own fate and that of the sword were intertwined.

The Runes on the Sword are the Worms that are wise—The Name of the Sword is the same as the Scythe.

Here the first part was easier to understand than the second. It merely meant that some kind of wisdom was written on the blade. And it was just possible that the Scythe referred to was nothing more than the same scythe that Death was said to wield.

But I still knew no more than I had known before. It seemed that I must decide to take up the sword again without being told why I had originally decided to put it down ...

There was a knock on the cabin door. Thinking it was the girl again, I cried out: 'I do not wish to be disturbed.'

'It is Morgeg,' replied the one who had knocked. 'Bishop Belphig instructed me to tell you that the sea-stag has been sighted. The hunt is about to begin.'

'I will come in a moment.'

I heard Morgeg's footfalls fade. I put my helm on my head, took up my axe and my spear and went to the door.

Perhaps the excitement of the hunt would drive some of my confusion away.

Belphig seemed to have regained all his old bland confidence. He was in full armour, his visor raised, and Morgeg now wore armour, too.

'Well, Count Urlik, we shall soon have the diversion we actually sought when we originally set out, eh?' He slapped the rail with his gauntleted hand.

The wheels of the ship were moving comparatively slowly over the viscous ocean and the sea-beasts pulling the gigantic sea-chariot were swimming at an almost leisurely rate.

'The sea-stag's horns broke the surface near by a while ago,' Morgeg said. 'The beast must be quite near. It has no gills and must eventually surface again. That is when we must be ready to strike.' He indicated the warriors lining the rails above the ship's hull. They all held long, heavy harpoons, each with up to ten cruel barbs.

'Is the beast likely to attack?' I asked.

'Have no fear,' Bishop Belphig said. 'We are safe enough up here.'

'I came for the excitement,' I told him. 'I would experience it.'

He shrugged. 'Very well. Morgeg, will you escort Count Urlik to the lower deck.'

Spear and axe in hand I followed Morgeg down the several companionways to the lower deck and emerged to discover that the sea-chariot's wheels had stopped almost completely.

Morgeg craned his neck and peered into the gloom. 'Ah,' he said. And he pointed.

I had the impression of antlers very much like those of the stags I had seen on John Daker's world. I had no means, however, of judging their size.

I wondered if this were some land beast that had taken to the sea just as the seals had returned to the land. Or perhaps it was another hybrid, bred centuries before by Rowernarc's scientists.

The atmosphere on the great chariot was tense. The antlers seemed to be coming closer, as if to inspect the strangers who had intruded into its province.

I moved nearer to the rail, a warrior making room for me.

Morgeg murmured 'I will return to my master's side.' And he left me.

I heard a snort—a gigantic snort. This beast was plainly larger than an ordinary stag!

Now I could see red eyes glaring at us. A huge, bovine face emerged from the twilight, its nostrils dilating and contracting. It snorted again and this time I felt its breath strike my face.

In silence, the harpooners prepared for its charge.

I looked up at the prow, noticing that the *slevahs* had submerged, as if they wanted no part of this madness ...

The sea-stag bellowed, raising its massive body from the viscous waters. The thick, saline liquid ran in streamers down its coarse, oily pelt and I saw that its muscular forelegs were, in fact, flippers terminating in a clublike appendage that only barely recalled the hoof of a true stag. These flippers it now thrashed in the air, then sank down into the sea again, re-emerging a moment later with lowered head to charge our chariot.

From the top deck Morgeg's voice came:

'Let fly with the first harpoons!'

A third of the warriors flung back their arms and hurled their heavy lances at the advancing beast. The horns were almost fifteen feet long, with an even longer span.

Some of the harpoons flew past the sea-stag and lay for a moment on the surface of the water before sinking, others buried themselves in the body of the stag. But none struck the head and while it screamed with pain, it paused only for a moment before continuing its charge.

'Let fly with the second harpoons!'

The second wave of lances flew out. Two struck the horns and clattered harmlessly off them. Two struck the body but were shaken out by a twist of the animal's shoulders. The horns struck the chariot and sharp bone met metal with an awful clangour. The ship rocked, threatened to topple, righted itself on its flat, lower hull. One of the horns swept along the rail and, shrieking, several harpooners were hurled overboard, their armour gashed. I leaned over to see if they could be helped, but they were already sinking, as a man sinks in quicksand, some holding up their arms pleadingly, though their eyes spoke of the hopelessness of help.

This was a brutal, disgusting business, particularly since the instigator of the hunt was at the top of the ship in a relatively safe position.

Now the dripping head loomed over us and we staggered back as it opened its mouth to show teeth half the size of a large man's height, a red, curling tongue.

Dwarfed by the monster, I took up my stance on the swaying deck, drew back the arm holding my own spear and flung it into that open mouth. Its point entered the flesh of the gullet and the mouth instantly closed as, in agony, the beast backed off, moving its jaw from side to side as it tried to rid itself of the thing inside it.

One of the harpooners clapped me on the back as we saw dark blood begin to run from the sea-stag's snout.

From far above came the bland voice of Bishop Belphig. 'Well done, Sir Champion!'

At that moment I would rather the spear had entered Belphig's heart than the gullet of the monster whose territory we had invaded.

I grabbed up a harpoon from where it had been dropped by one of the men who had been swept overboard. I aimed again for the head, but the point struck the base of the left horn and dropped harmlessly into the sea.

The monster coughed and bits of the shaft of my spear were spewed out, some of them striking the ship's superstructure.

Then it charged again.

This time, as if encouraged by my partial success, one of the harpooners managed to drive his weapon into the sea-stag's flesh just below the right eye. A terrible scream came from the injured throat and, admitting defeat, the beast turned and began to swim away.

I drew a sigh of relief, but I had not reckoned with Bishop Belphig's bloodlust.

'Pursue it—quickly. It is making for its lair!' he cried.

The drivers lashed the sea-beasts to the surface, jerked on the ropes that were their reins and, using the long goads, turned them in pursuit of the disappearing stag.

'This is insanity! Let the thing go!' I shouted.

'What—and return to Rowernarc without a trophy!' screamed back the bishop. 'Give chase, whipmen. Give chase!'

The wheels began to whirl over the water again as we pursued our wounded quarry.

One of the harpooners gave me a sardonic look. 'They say our Lord Spiritual prefers slaughter to fornication.' He rubbed at his face. Blood spat by the stag had covered him.

'I do not know if he understands the difference any longer,' I said. 'Where is the monster heading?'

'Sea-stags make their lairs in caves. There is probably a small island near by. Our friend will head for that.'

'Have they no herds?'

'At certain times. But this is not their herding season. That is why it is relatively safe to hunt them. A herd, even mainly of cows, would quickly finish us.'

Two of the wheels on our side of the ship had been badly battered and the sea-chariot lurched unevenly as it sped over the ocean. The *slevahs* must have been even more powerful than the sea-stag to be able to cut through those thick waters and draw the heavy craft behind them.

The horns of the stag were still in sight through the gloom and, just ahead of that, the outline of a spike of obsidian rock, doubtless of the same range as the mountain from which Rowernarc had been carved.

'There!' The harpooner pointed. Grimly he hefted his barbed lance.

I bent and took the remaining harpoon off the deck.

Morgeg's distant voice shouted: 'Prepare!'

The stag had disappeared, but the tiny island of glassy rock could clearly be seen. The sea-chariot slewed round as the sea-beasts avoided dashing themselves on to the rock. We saw the black mouth of a cave.

We had found the monster's lair.

From within the cave came an almost pathetic snort of pain. And then came the astonishing order from above

'Prepare to disembark!'

Belphig meant his men to enter the cave armed only with their harpoons!

CHAPTER NINE

THE SLAUGHTERING IN THE CAVE

And so we disembarked.

All save Belphig, his entourage and the whipmen in the prow, began to wade through the clinging shallows and gain a slippery foothold on the rock. I had my battle-axe crooked in one arm, the barbed harpoon held at my side in the other hand. Belphig watched and waved from the top deck.

'Good luck, Count Urlik. If you kill the stag it will be

65

another great deed to add to your long list . . .'

I thought the whole nature of the hunt was useless and cruel, but I felt I must go with the others to finish what we had begun—either to kill the monster or be killed by it.

With some difficulty we clambered around the rock until we had reached the mouth of the cave. A terrible stench was issuing from it, as if the beast had already begun to rot.

The man who had spoken earlier now said: 'That's the stink of its dung. The sea-stag is not a clean beast.'

Now I felt even more reluctant to enter the cave.

Another bellow came, as the stag scented us.

The harpooners hung back nervously. No man wished to be the first into the lair.

At last, dry-mouthed but desperate, I elbowed my way forward, took a good grip on my harpoon and stepped into the black maw.

The stench was nauseating and I felt I would choke on it. There was a heavy movement and I thought I saw the outline of one of the stag's great antlers. A rapid snorting came from the thing's nostrils then. I heard its gigantic flippers thud on the floor. I had the impression of a long, sinuous body ending in a wide, flat tail.

The rest of the men were following me. From one of them I took a brand and touched the stud in its handle. Faint light illuminated the cavern.

The shadow of the sea-stag was what I saw first and then I saw the beast himself, on my right, pressed against the wall, blood pouring from its wounds, its massive body looking even larger on land than it had in the sea.

It hauled itself about on its giant flippers. It lowered its head menacingly but it did not charge. It was warning us away. It was giving us the chance to leave without a fight.

I was tempted to recall the men—lead them from the cave—but I had no authority over them. Bishop Belphig was their master and he would punish them if they did not obey him.

So, knowing that this would incense the beast, I hurled my harpoon at its left eye.

It turned its head just as the lance left my hand and the weapon grazed its snout.

It charged.

There was confusion then. Men screamed, tried to dodge, tried to get a clear cast at it, backed away, were impaled on its antlers.

When it raised its head three men hung on its horns, their bodies completely pierced. Two were dead. One was dying. Small moans came from his lips.

There was nothing I could do to save him. The stag shook its great head, trying to dislodge the corpses, but they remained where they were.

An idea began to form in my mind.

But then the stag lowered its head and charged again. I jumped aside, striking out with my long-hafted battle-axe and cutting a deep groove in its left shoulder. It turned towards me, its teeth snapping, its red eyes glaring in a mixture of anguish and surprise. I struck it another blow and it withdrew its bleeding snout. Again it shook its horns and now one of the torn bodies fell limply to the filthy floor of the cave. The stag nudged at it awkwardly with a flipper.

I looked for the remaining harpooners. They were huddled near the cave entrance.

The stag was now between me and the others. The cave was lit still by two brands which had fallen to the floor. I retreated into the shadows. The stag saw the others, lowered its head again and charged.

I was knocked flat by its huge fish tail as it moved past.

The beast bellowed as the harpooners scattered. I heard their cries as they were caught on its horns, as they plunged into the thick waters, seeking to escape.

And now I was alone in the cave.

The sea-stag began to scrape its horns on the edges of the cave mouth, scraping off human flesh.

I decided that I was as good as dead. How could I defeat such a monster alone? Its body blocked the entrance—my only chance of escape. Sooner or later it would remember I was there, or possibly scent me.

I kept as still as possible. The stink of ordure clogged my mouth and nostrils. I had no harpoon with which to defend myself, only the axe—an unsuitable weapon for dealing with a giant sea-stag . . .

Once again the beast opened its bovine snout and sent up a huge bellowing. Then the noise dropped as it moaned to itself.

Would it decide to enter the sea again? To heal its wounds in the salt?

I waited tensely for it to decide. But then there was another rattle of harpoons against rock and antlers and the monster screamed and backed into the cave.

Again I was forced to dodge its tail.

I prayed that the harpooners would return—at least long enough to give me the chance to get past the stag to a safer position.

The stag snorted, dragging its whale-like body first one way and then another across the floor of the cave, as it, too, expected the arrival of the warriors.

But nothing happened.

Did they think me dead?

Were they abandoning the chase?

I listened for shouts, but heard nothing.

Another bellow. Another movement of the unnatural body.

I began to edge along the wall of the cave, moving as softly as possible.

I was half-way to the cave-mouth when my foot struck a yielding object. It was the corpse of one of the harpooners. I lifted my leg to step over the thing but my foot then caught on a piece of loose armour and sent it clattering across the obsidian floor.

The beast snorted and turned its baleful eyes to regard me.

I stood stock still, hoping it would not realise that I lived.

It shook its horns again and dragged its body round.

My mouth and throat were dry.

It raised its muzzle and bellowed, its lips curling back from its huge teeth. Blood now encrusted those lips and it was plainly half blind in one eye.

Then, horrifyingly, it raised its body up and its strange flippers with their club-like appendages, thrashed at the air, fell back to the ground, shook the floor of the cavern.

The antlers were lowered.

The stag charged.

I saw the huge horns bearing down on me and I had seen how they could impale a man. I flung my body flat against the wall and to one side. The antlers crashed within inches of my right shoulder and the stag's massive forehead—as wide as my body was long—was a foot from my face.

The idea I had had earlier came back to me. I believed there was only one chance of defeating the monster.

I jumped.

I leapt towards that forehead, grabbed the oily pelt, literally ran up its snout and then wrapped my legs and one arm around the branches of the left antler.

The beast was puzzled. I do not think it realised I was there. I raised the axe.

The stag looked about the cavern for me, still snorting.

I brought the axe down.

It bit deep into his skull. He roared and screamed and shook his head rapidly from side to side. But I had expected this and I clung to the branches as tenaciously as was possible, striking again at the exact place I had struck before.

I split the bone. A little blood came. But all this served to do was to make the stag's movements more frantic. Its body sliding behind it, it waddled on its flippers, moving rapidly about the cave, scraping its antlers on roof and walls, trying to dislodge me.

But I hung on.

And I struck again.

This time pieces of bone flew into the air and a stream of blood poured from the skull.

Another fearsome bellow which became a scream of rage and terror.

Another blow.

The axe haft snapped with the force of my striking and I was left holding nothing but a piece of broken pole.

But the blade had buried itself in the brain.

The bulk of the stag crashed to the floor as the strength went out of the flippers.

It moaned pathetically. It tried to rise.

With a spluttering noise the last mixture of breath and blood left its body.

The head fell to one side and I fell with it, leaping free just as the antlers reached the floor.

The sea-stag was dead. I had killed it single-handed.

I tried to tug the broken haft of the axe out of the beast's head, but it was buried too deep. I left my axe there and stumbled, half dazed, from the mouth of the cave.

'It is over,' I said. 'Your quarry is vanquished.'

I felt no pride in my accomplishment. I looked towards the ship.

But no ship was there.

Bishop Belphig's sea-chariot had rolled away, presumably back to Rowernarc—doubtless because they thought me dead.

'Belphig!' I shouted, hoping my voice would carry over the waters where my eye could not see. 'Morgeg! I am alive! I have killed the stag!'

But there was no reply.

I looked at the low, brown clouds. At the murky, moody ocean.

I had been abandoned in the middle of a nightmare sea through which, as Belphig had said, no ships passed. I was alone save for the corpses of the harpooners, the carcass of the sea-stag.

Panic seized me.

'BELPHIG! COME BACK!'

A slight echo. Nothing more.

'I AM ALIVE!'

And the echo seemed stronger this time and it seemed sardonic.

I could not stay alive for long on that bleak sliver of rock which was less than fifty yards across. I stumbled up the sides, climbing as high as I could. But what point was there in that when the twilight sea had no horizon that was not obscured on all sides by the brown cloudbanks?

I sat down on a small ledge, the only reasonably flat surface on the entire rock.

I was trembling. I was afraid.

The air seemed to grow colder and I drew my coat about me but it would not keep out the chill that grasped my bones, my liver, my heart.

An immortal I might be. A phoenix for ever reborn. A wanderer in eternity.

But if I was to die here, that dying would seem to take an eternity. If I were a phoenix, then I was a phoenix trapped in obsidian as a fly is trapped in amber.

At that thought all my courage went out of me and I contemplated my fate with nothing but despair.

BOOK THREE

Visions and Revelations

Destiny's Champion,
Fate's Fool.
Eternity's Soldier,
Time's Tool.
    —The Chronicle of the Black Sword

CHAPTER ONE

THE LAUGHING DWARF

The fight with the sea-stag had so exhausted me that, after a while, I fell asleep with my back against the rock and my legs stretched before me on the ledge.

When I awoke it was with some of my courage returned, though I could see no easy solution to my plight.

From the mouth of the cave below the stench had increased as the stag's flesh began to rot. There was also an unpleasant slithering sound. Peering over the edge I saw that small snake-like creatures were wriggling into the cave in their thousands. Doubtless these were the carrion eaters of the sea. Hundreds of black bodies were tangled together as they moved up the rock to where the sea-stag lay.

Any thought I might have entertained of using the stag's carcass as meat to sustain me disappeared completely. I hoped the disgusting creatures would finish their meal quickly and leave. At least there were harpoons in the cave. As soon as I could reach them I would gather them up. They would be useful for defence against any other monster that might lurk in these waters and there might also be fish of some kind in the shallows, though I rather doubted it.

It occurred to me that Bishop Belphig might have planned to maroon me all along, simply because my questions were embarrassing him.

Had he planned the hunt with that in mind? If so, by going with the men into the sea-stag's lair, I had played completely into his hands.

For want of anything else to do, I made a circuit of the island. It did not take long. My first impression had been the right one. Nothing grew here. There was no drinkable water. The people of Rowernarc got their water from melting ice, but there was no ice on that jagged spur of obsidian.

The writhing carrion creatures were still entering the cavern which was now filled with a slithering and hissing as they fought over the carcass.

Momentarily a rent appeared in the bank of clouds overhead and the faint rays of the dying sun were reflected on the black waters.

I returned to my ledge. There was nothing to do until the carrion had finished their meal.

Hope of finding Ermizhad had waned, for it was unlikely I could ever return to Rowernarc. And if I died I might find myself in an incarnation worse than this one. I might not even remember Ermizhad, just as I could now not remember why the Black Sword was such an important factor in my destiny.

I remembered Ermizhad's lovely face. I recalled the beauty of the planet to which I had brought tranquillity at the cost of genocide.

I began to doze again and soon I was no longer alone, for the familiar visions and voices returned. I fought to drive them from my brain, keeping my eyes open and staring into the gloom. But soon the visions imposed themselves against the clouds and the sea, the words seemed to come from all sides.

'Leave me in peace,' I begged. 'Let me die in peace!'

The slithering and hissing from the cavern of death mingled with the whispers and the echoes of the ghostly voices.

'Leave me alone!'

I was like a child, frightened by the things it imagines in the dark. My voice was the impotent pleading of a child.

'Please leave me alone!'

I heard laughter. It was low, sardonic laughter and it seemed to come from above. I looked up.

Once again a dream seemed to have assumed physical reality, for I saw the figure quite clearly. It was climbing down the rock towards me.

It was a dwarf with bandy legs and a light beard. Its face was young and its eyes bright with humour.

72

'Greetings,' it said.

'Greetings,' I replied. 'Now vanish, I beg you.'

'But I have come to pass the time with you.'

'You are a creature of my imagination.'

'I resent that. Besides, you must have an unpleasant imagination if you can create so poor a thing as myself. I am Jermays the Crooked. Do you not remember me?'

'Why should I remember you?'

'Oh, we have met once or twice before. Like you, I have no existence in time as most people understand it—as you once understood it, if my memory serves. I have been of assistance to you in the past.'

'Mock me not, phantom.'

'Sir Champion, I am not a phantom. At least, not much of one. True I live for the most part in the shadow worlds, the worlds which have little true substance. A trick played on me by the gods that made me the crooked thing I am.'

'Gods?'

Jermays winked. 'Those who claim to be gods. Though they're as much slaves of fate as we are. Gods—powers—superior entities—they are called many things. And we, I suppose, are demi-gods—the tools of the gods.'

'I have no time for mystical speculation of that kind.'

'My dear Champion, at this moment you have time for anything. Are you hungry?'

'You know that I am.'

The dwarf reached into his green jerkin and pulled out half a loaf of bread. He handed it to me. It seemed substantial enough. I bit it. It seemed quite real. I ate it and I felt my stomach filled.

'I thank you,' I said. 'If I am to go mad, then this seems the best way.'

Jermays sat beside me on the ledge, resting the spear he carried against the rock. He smiled. 'You are certain my face is not familiar?'

'I have never seen you before.'

'Strange. But then perhaps our temporal identities are in different phases and you have not yet met me, though I have met you.'

'Quite possible.'

Jermays had a wine-skin hanging on his belt. He unhooked it, took a swig and handed it to me.

The wine was good. I drank sparely and gave him back the skin.

'I see you do not have your sword with you,' he commented.

I gave him a searching look, but there seemed no irony in his voice. 'I have lost it,' I said.

He laughed heartily. 'Lost it! Lost that black blade! Oh, ho! ho! ho! You are making fun of me, Sir Champion.'

I frowned impatiently. 'It is true. What do you know of the Black Sword?'

'What all know. It is a sword that has possessed many names, as you have possessed many names. It has appeared in different guises, just as your physical appearance is not always the same. They say it was forged by the Forces of Darkness for the one destined to be their champion, but that is a rather unsophisticated view, wouldn't you agree?'

'I would.'

'The Black Sword is said to exist on many planes and it is also said to have a twin. Once when I knew you you were called Elrik and the blade was called *Stormbringer*—its twin *Mournblade*. However, some say that the duality is an illusion, that there is only one Black Sword and that it existed before the gods, before Creation.'

'These are legends,' I said. 'They do not explain the nature of the thing at all. I have been told it is my destiny to bear it, yet I refuse. Does that mean ought to you?'

'It means that you must be an unhappy man. The Champion and the Sword are One. If man betrays blade or blade betrays man, then a great crime is committed.'

'Why is this so?'

Jermays shrugged and smiled. 'I know not. The gods know not. It has always been. Believe me, Sir Champion, it is the same as asking what created the universes through which you and I move so freely.'

'Is there any means of staying on one plane, on one world?'

Jermays pursed his lips. 'I have never considered the problem. It suits me to travel as I do.' He grinned. 'But, then, I am not a Hero.'

'Have you heard of a place called Tanelorn?'

'Aye. You might call it a veteran's town.' He rubbed his long nose and winked. 'It's said to be in the domain of the Grey Lords, those who serve neither Law nor Chaos . . .'

A faint memory stirred. 'What do you mean by Law and Chaos?'

'Some call them Light and Darkness. Again there are disputes among philosophers and the like as to what defines them. Others believe that they are one—part of the same force. On different worlds, in different times, they believe different things. And what they believe, I suppose, is true.'

'But where is Tanelorn?'

'Where? A strange question for you to ask. Tanelorn is always there.'

I rose impatiently. 'Are you part of my torment, Master Jermays? You further complicate the riddles.'

'Untrue, Sir Champion. But you ask impossible questions of me. Perhaps a wiser being could tell you more, but I cannot. I am not a philosopher or a hero—I am just Jermays the Crooked.' His smile wavered and I saw sadness in his eyes.

'I am sorry,' I said. I sighed. 'But I feel there is no solution to my dilemma. How did you get to this place?'

'A gap in the fabric of another world. I do not know how I go from plane to plane, but I do and there it is.'

'Can you leave?'

'I will, when it is time to leave. But I do not know when that will be.'

'I see.' I peered out at the gloomy sea.

Jermays wrinkled his nose. 'I have seen few places as unpleasant as this. I can see why you should want to leave. Perhaps if you took up the Black Sword again ...?'

'No!'

He was startled. 'Forgive me. I did not comprehend that you were so adamant about the matter.'

I spread my hands. 'Something spoke from within me. Something that refuses—at all costs—to accept the Black Sword.'

'Then you ...'

Jermays was gone.

Again I was alone. Again I wondered if he had been an illusion, if my whole experience here was an illusion, if this entire thing were not some event taking place in the sleeping or insane brain of John Daker ...

The air before me suddenly shivered and became bright. It was as if I looked through a window into another world. I moved towards the window but it always remained the same distance from me.

I peered through the window and I saw Ermizhad. She looked back at me.

'Erekosë?'

'Ermizhad. I will return to you.'

'You cannot, Erekosë, until you have taken up the Black Sword again . . .'

And the window closed and I saw only the dark sea again.

I roared my rage to the lowering sky.

'Whoever you are who has done this thing to me—I will have my vengeance on you!'

My words were absorbed by stark silence.

I knelt upon the ledge and sobbed.

'CHAMPION!'

A bell tolled. The voice called.

'CHAMPION!'

I stared about and saw nothing.

'CHAMPION!'

Now a whisper: '*Black Sword. Black Sword. Black Sword.*'

'*No!*'

'*You avoid the destiny for which you were created. Take up the Black Sword again, Champion. Take it up and know glory!*'

'*I know only misery and guilt. I will not wield the Sword.*'

'*You will.*'

The statement was a positive one. It had no threat in it, only certainty.

The slithering carrion had retreated to the sea. I made my way down to the cave and discovered the bones of the mighty sea-stag, the skeletons of my companions. The huge skull with its proud antlers regarded me as if in accusation. Quickly I found the harpoons, wrenched my broken axe from the skull and retreated back to my ledge.

I frowned, remembering the sword of Erekosë. That strange, poisoned blade had seemed powerful enough. I had had little reluctance to wield it. But perhaps that sword had been, as Jermays had hinted, merely an aspect of the Black Sword. I shrugged the thought off.

On my ledge, I arranged my weapons about me and waited for another vision.

Sure enough, it came.

It was a large raft, fashioned rather like a huge sleigh and reminiscent, in ornament, of the sea-chariot that had brought me here. But this was not drawn by sea-beasts. Instead it was pulled over the waters by birds that were like overgrown herons covered not by feathers but with dull, gleaming scales.

There was a group of men aboard the sleigh, dressed in heavy furs and mail armour, carrying swords and spears.

'Go away!' I shouted. 'Leave me in peace!'

They did not heed me, but turned their weird craft towards the rock.

I picked up the battle-axe by its broken haft. This time, I decided, hallucination or not, I would drive my tormentors away or perish in the attempt.

Now someone was calling to me and the voice seemed familiar. I knew I had heard it in one of my dreams.

'Count Urlik! Count Urlik—is that you?'

The speaker had thrown back his fur hood to reveal a shock of red hair, a young, handsome face.

'Begone!' I cried. 'I will listen to no more riddles!'

The face seemed puzzled.

The scaly herons turned in the sky and the baroque sleigh bounced closer. I stood on my ledge, my battle-axe held threateningly in my hand.

'Begone!'

But the herons were over my head. They settled on the top of the crag and folded their leathery wings. From the sleigh the red-haired man jumped, the others following. His arms were spread wide. His face held a grin of relief.

'Count Urlik. We have found you at last. We expected you at the Scarlet Fjord many days since!'

I did not lower my guard.

'Who are you?' I said.

'Why I am Bladrak Morningspear. I am the Hound of the Scarlet Fjord!'

Still I was wary.

'And why are you here?'

He put his hands on his hips and laughed uncertainly. His fur robe fell away to reveal muscular arms on which barbaric golden bracelets were twined.

'We have been seeking you, my lord. Did you not hear the bell?'

'I heard a bell, aye.'

'It was the Bell of Urlik. The Lady of the Chalice told us it would bring you to us to help in our war against the Silver

77

Warriors.'

I slightly relaxed my grip on the broken haft. Then these people really were of this world. But why had Belphig feared them? Now, at least, it seemed, I would find an answer to some of the mysteries.

'Will you return with us, my lord, to the Scarlet Fjord? Will you come aboard our boat?'

Warily, I left the ledge and approached him.

I do not know how many days or hours I had been on the sea-stag's island, but I suppose I made a peculiar appearance. My eyes were probably wild and wary, like those of a madman, and I clung to a broken axe as if it were the only thing in the world I trusted.

Bladrak was puzzled but he kept his good humour. He spread one hand out to indicate the boat. 'We are relieved to see you, Count Urlik of the Frozen Keep. It is almost too late. We hear the Silver Warriors plan a massive attack on the southern shore.'

'Rowernarc?'

'Aye, Rowernarc and the other settlements.'

'Are you enemies of Rowernarc?'

He smiled. 'Well, we are not allies. But let us make haste to return. I will tell you more when we are safe in port. These are dangerous waters.'

I nodded. 'I have discovered that.'

Some of the men had been inspecting the cave. They came out, lugging the massive skull of the slain sea-stag.

'Look, Bladrak,' one called. 'It has been killed by an axe.'

Bladrak raised his eyebrows and looked at me. 'Your axe?'

I nodded. 'I had nothing against the poor beast. It was really Belphig's quarry.'

Bladrak threw back his head and laughed. 'Look, friends,' he called, pointing at me, 'there is proof we have our Hero!'

Still somewhat dazed I entered the boat and took my place on one of the benches bolted to the bottom. Bladrak sat beside me. 'Let's be away,' he said.

The men who had found the sea-stag's skull hastily dumped it in the back of the boat and clambered aboard. Some of them jerked on the heron's reins and they took to the air again.

Suddenly the boat lunged forward and was flying across the dark sea.

Bladrak looked back. The giant skull had been placed so that it covered a long, slender box which was, in contrast to everything else aboard, completely without ornament. 'Be careful of the box,' he said.

'The bell you sounded,' I said. 'Did it toll just recently?'

'Aye—we tried again, since you had not come. Then the Lady of the Chalice said that you were somewhere on the Great Salt Sea and so we went looking for you.'

'When did you first summon me?'

'Some sixty days ago.'

'I went to Rowernarc,' I said.

'And Belphig captured you?'

'Perhaps. Yes, I suspect that is what he did. Though I did not know it at the time. What do you know of Belphig, Sir Bladrak?'

'Little enough. He has always been an enemy of the free sailors.'

'Are you those whom he called pirates?'

'Oh, doubtless, aye. Traditionally we have lived by raiding the ships and cities of the softer folk along the coast. But now we give our full attention to the Silver Warriors. With you to aid us we stand some chance of beating them, though time is very short.'

'I hope you do not rely too much on me, Bladrak Morning-spear. I have no supernatural powers, I assure you.'

He laughed. 'You are very modest for a hero. But I know what you mean—you are without weapons. All that has been dealt with by the Lady of the Chalice.' He flung his hand backward to indicate the slender box in the stern. 'See, my lord, we have brought your sword for you!'

CHAPTER TWO

THE SCARLET FJORD

At Bladrak's words a great sense of dread filled me. I stared at him in horror, hardly able to comprehend what had happened.

I had been manipulated into this situation and Bladrak had been an unknowing agent of this trick.

Bladrak was taken aback. 'What is it, my lord? Have we done wrong? Have we done something that will bring doom upon you?'

My voice was hoarse and I hardly knew the words I spoke

for, consciously, I still had no idea of the Black Sword's nature. 'Doom on us all, Bladrak Morningspear, in some form or other. Aye, and perhaps the accomplishment of what you desire. Do you know the price?'

'Price?'

My face twisted. I flung my hands to cover it.

'What price is that, Count Urlik?'

I cleared my throat but still did not look at him. 'I do not know, Bladrak. That, in time, we shall both discover. As for now, I wish that sword kept away from me. I do not want the box opened.'

'We will do all you desire, Count Urlik. But you will lead us, will you not, against the Silver Warriors?'

'I nodded. If that was why I was called, that is what I will do.'

'Without the sword?'

'Without the sword.'

I said nothing further on our journey to Bladrak's home, but sometimes, involuntarily, my eyes strayed to the black box which lay beneath the staring skull of the slain sea-stag. Then I would twist my head away and my melancholy would suffuse my brain.

Then, at last, tall cliffs loomed out of the clouds. Massive, black, they were even more unwelcoming than the obsidian crags of Rowernarc.

Hanging over a part of this range I detected a rosy glow and I stared at it in curiosity.

'What is that?' I asked Bladrak.

He smiled. 'The Scarlet Fjord. We are about to enter it.'

We were very close to the cliffs, but we did not alter course. The herons flew directly towards them. Then I saw why. There was a gap between two and deep water filled it. This must be the entrance to the fjord. One of Bladrak's men raised a huge, curling horn to his lips and blew a wild blast upon it. From above came an answering blast and, looking up, I saw that there were battlements carved on both sides of the narrow opening and at the battlements stood warriors.

It was so dark between the cliffs that I thought we must surely be dashed to pieces, but the herons guided us around a bend and then I blinked in wonder. The water was scarlet. The air was scarlet. The rock shone with a deep, ruby colour, and the fjord was full of warmth.

The warm, red light issued from the mouths of a thousand caves which honeycombed the eastern wall of the fjord.

'What are those fires?' I asked.

Bladrak shook his head. 'None know. They have been there for ever. Some believe them to be volcanic, others say that ancient scientists invented a peculiar kind of fire which fed on rock and air alone, but when they had invented it they had no use for it. They could not put it out, so they buried it. And the Scarlet Fjord was born.'

I could not keep my gaze off the wonder of those burning cliffs. Everything was bathed in the same red light. I felt truly warmed for the first time since I had arrived.

Bladrak indicated the western and southern walls of the fjord. 'That is where we live.'

Carved where the cliffs met the water were long quays. At these quays were tied many boats of a similar design to that in which we sailed. Above the quays were ramps and steps and terraces. Plain, square doorways had been cut from the rock and outside them now stood hosts of men, women and children, all dressed in simple, plain-coloured smocks, tabards and dresses.

When they saw us head for the southern quay they began to cheer. Then they began to chant.

It was one word they chanted.

'Urlik! Urlik! Urlik!'

Bladrak raised his arms to them, begging for silence, his grin widening as they only reluctantly subsided.

'Friends of the Scarlet Fjord! Free folk of the South! Bladrak has returned with Count Urlik who will save us. Look!' He pointed dramatically first at the sea-stag's skull and then at my broken axe. 'With that axe alone he killed the Bellyripper. Thus will we destroy the Silver Warriors who enslave our brothers of the North!'

And this time the cheer, to my embarrassment, was even louder. I resolved to tell Bladrak as soon as possible that I had not been solely responsible for slaying the stag.

The boat was berthed and we stepped on to the quay. Rosy-cheeked women approached us and embraced Bladrak, curtsied to me.

I could not help but notice the contrast between these folk and the neurasthenic people of Rowernarc, with their pale skins and their unhealthy appetites. Perhaps it was that the folk of Rowernarc were over-civilised and could only think of the future, while the dwellers of the Scarlet Fjord lived in the present, concerning themselves with immediate problems.

And the immediate problem of these people was plainly the threat of the Silver Warriors.

At least, I told myself, I would not now be dealing with the evasions of a Bishop Belphig. Bladrak would tell me everything he knew.

The so-called Hound of the Scarlet Fjord led me into his apartments. They were comfortably furnished and lit by lamps that also shone with a rosy glow. The decoration of the furniture and wall-hangings more closely resembled those that I had seen on my chariot and my weapons when I had found myself on the frozen plain.

I sat down thankfully in a chair carved from solid amber and surprisingly comfortable. Many of the furnishings were in amber and the table itself was carved from a solid block of quartz.

I could not help reflecting on the irony that if Man's history had begun with the Stone Age it was about to end with a Stone Age, also.

The food was simple but tasty and I learned from Bladrak that this, like that of Rowernarc, was grown in special gardens in the deepest caves.

When we had eaten, we sat with our wine-cups and said nothing for a while.

Then I spoke.

'Bladrak. You must assume that my memory is poor and answer even the simplest questions I ask you. I have endured much of late and it has made me forgetful.'

'I understand,' he said. 'What do you wish to know?'

'First, exactly how I was summoned.'

'You know that you slept in the Frozen Keep, far away on the South Ice?'

'I know that I found myself on the South Ice, riding in a chariot towards the coast.'

'Aye—heading for the Scarlet Fjord. But as you came along the coast you were diverted at Rowernarc.'

'That explains much,' I said, 'for I could find no one there who admitted to summoning me. Indeed, some, like Belphig, seemed to resent me.'

'Aye, and they held you there until they could maroon you on the island we found you on.'

'Perhaps that was their intention. I am not sure. But why Belphig should wish to do such a thing is hard to say.'

'The brains of the folk of Rowernarc are'—Bladrak gestured at his head with his finger—'addled—askew—I know not—something...'

'But Belphig must have known of the bell, for when it sounded a second time he turned the ship about and your name was mentioned. That means that they knew you were summoning me. And they did not tell me. Why did the bell sound over the sea? And why did I not hear a bell the first time, only a voice.'

Bladrak looked at his beaker. 'They say the bell speaks with a human voice across the planes of the universe, but only sounds like a bell on this plane. I do not know if that is true, for I have only heard it ring in the ordinary way.'

'Where is the bell?'

'I know not. We pray, the bell rings. The Lady of the Chalice told us that.'

'Who is the Lady of the Chalice? Does she appear with a gigantic golden cup which screams?'

'Nay...' Bladrak gave me a sideways look. 'That is just her name. She came to us when the danger of the Silver Warriors grew great. She said there was a hero who would help us. She said he was Urlik Skarsol, Count of the White Wastes, Lord of the Frozen Keep, Prince of the Southern Ice, Master of the Cold Sword...'

'The *Cold* Sword? Not the Black Sword?'

'The Cold Sword.'

'Continue.'

'The Lady of the Chalice said that if we called the hero urgently enough it would sound Urlik's Bell which would summon him. He would come to our aid, he would take up the Cold Sword and the blood of the Silver Warriors would fill the Chalice and feed the Sun.'

I sighed. I supposed that the Cold Sword was the local name for the Black Sword. Jermays had said the sword had many names on many worlds. But something within me was still resolute.

'We shall have to manage against the Silver Warriors without the sword,' I said firmly. 'Now tell me who these warriors are.'

'They came from nowhere a year or so since. It is believed that they are Moonites whose own home grew too cold to support them. They have a cruel queen it is said, but none has ever seen her. They are virtually invulnerable to ordinary weapons and therefore well-nigh invincible in battle. They easily took the cities of the Northern coast, one after the other. Most of the people there, like those of Rowernarc, are too self-absorbed to know what happens to them. But the Silver Warriors have enslaved them and put them to death and made them brainless, inhuman creatures. We are the free sailors, we lived off the soft citizens, but now we rescue those we can and bring them here. For some while that is what we have been doing. But now all the signs show that the Silver Warriors are planning to attack the Southern coasts. In a direct fight we could not possibly defeat them. Soon the whole race will be enslaved.'

'Are these warriors of flesh and blood?' I asked, for I had the notion that they might be robots or androids of some kind.

'Aye, they are of flesh and blood. They are tall and thin and arrogant and speak rarely and wear that strange silver armour. Their faces, too, are silver, as are their hands. We have seen no other parts of their bodies.'

'You have never captured one?'

'Never. Their armour burns us when we touch it.'

I frowned.

'And what do you want me to do?' I asked.

'Lead us. Be our Hero.'

'But you seem well equipped to lead your folk.'

'I am. But we are dealing here with some beyond our usual experience. You are a Hero—you can anticipate more things than can we.'

'I hope you are right,' I said. 'I hope you are right, Sir Bladrak of the Scarlet Fjord.'

CHAPTER THREE

THE RAID ON NALANARC

Bladrak informed me that an expedition against the Silver Warriors was already planned for the next day. The ships had been prepared for it and he had been awaiting my arrival before setting off against the island of Nalanarc which lay a few miles distant from the Northwestern coast. The object of the raid was not to kill the Silver Warriors, but to rescue the prisoners they had on the island. Bladrak was not sure what the prisoners were being used for, but he suspected they were engaged in making ships and weapons for the attack the Silver Warriors planned on the Southern coast shortly.

'How do you know they plan this attack?' I asked.

'We got the news from some of the slaves we rescued. Besides, it's been obvious to anyone who's been near 'em that they're planning the attack on the South. What would you do if you were a conqueror and were constantly raided from one particular area?'

'Set out to eliminate the source of my irritation,' I said.

When the great fleet sailed I sailed with it.

We left the waving, cheering women behind in the Scarlet Fjord, passed between the cliffs and were soon on the open sea.

Initially there was some confusion as the herons crossed some of their lines and had to be untangled, but this did not last long and soon we were heading north.

Bladrak was singing some obscure, symbolic chant that I doubt even he knew the meaning of. He seemed full of high spirits though I discovered he had made no specific plans for the raid, save to get there somehow and get the slaves off somehow.

I outlined a plan to him and he listened with keen interest. 'Very well,' he said, 'we'll try it.'

It was a simple enough plan and, not knowing the Silver Warriors, I had no idea if it would work or not.

We sped over the waters for some time, the runners of the sleds skipping over the thick surface.

Through the murk we passed until a large island could be seen ahead.

Now Bladrak shouted to his leading craft. 'Go in quickly, loose your weapons and then retreat. Wait for their own boats to follow and then lead them a dance while we get the slaves aboard in the confusion.'

That was my plan. I prayed it was a good one.

The leading craft acknowledged Bladrak's orders and sped ahead while the others slowed and waited in a bank of brown cloud.

Soon we heard a distant commotion, then we saw the ships of the Scarlet Fjord scudding away from the island. They were pursued by larger, heavier craft which seemed to be the first ships that actually moved through the waters, but I could not see, from that distance, what powered them.

Now we moved in.

The island of Nalanarc grew larger and larger and I could see through the twilight that there were buildings actually raised on parts of the place. Perhaps the Silver Warriors did not build habitually in the living stone as did Bladrak's and Rowernarc's people.

The buildings were square, squat, dimly lit from within. They were built down a hill, with a large building centrally placed at the top. At the bottom of the hill were the familiar openings to caverns.

'That is where the slaves are,' Bladrak told me. 'They are worked in those caverns building ships and weapons until they die, then a new batch replaces them. Men and women of all ages are there. They are hardly fed anything. There are always plenty more, you see. I do not think the Silver Warriors mean our folk to live once the world is theirs.'

While I was prepared to believe Bladrak, I had once before been told by those who had summoned me that the people they fought were unremittingly evil. I had discovered that the Eldren were in fact the victims. I wanted to see for myself what the Silver Warriors were doing.

The herons drew our boats up on to the island's beach and we piled out, heading for the caverns at the base of the hill.

It was plain that almost all the Silver Warriors had gone in pursuit of the few ships we had sent in ahead. I guessed it would not be a tactic we could use twice.

Into the caves we ran and I had my first sight of the warriors.

They were on average a good seven feet high, but extremely thin, with long arms and legs and narrow heads. Their skin was actually white, but with a faint silver sheen. Their armour covered their bodies, apparently without joins, and their heads were encased in tight-fitting helmets.

They were armed with long, double-bladed halberds. When they saw us, they came rushing at us with them. But they seemed somewhat clumsy with the halberds and I guessed they might be used to some other kind of weapon.

We had armed ourselves with what Bladrak had assured me were the only useful tools against the Silver Warriors whose armour could not be pierced and would burn whoever tried to handle it.

These weapons were wide-meshed nets which we flung at them as they approached. The nets clung to their bodies and tripped them and they could not free themselves.

I looked about the cavern workshops and was horrified by the condition of the naked men, women and children who had been set to labouring here.

'Get these people out as quickly as you can,' I said.

One Silver Warrior had not been entangled by a net. He came running at me with his halberd. I knocked it aside with my restored battle-axe and, heedless of the warning Bladrak had given me, chopped at his body.

A horrible jolt ran up my arms and sent me staggering. But the Silver Warrior had been toppled too.

I was incredulous. I knew I had received nothing less than an electric shock.

Now Bladrak and his men were herding the dazed slaves out of the caves towards the ships.

I looked up at the larger building on the top of the hill. I saw a glint of silver and I saw a shape that was familiar framed against a window.

It wa someone wearing the bulbous armour of Rowernarc.

Filled with curiosity and careless of the potential danger, I dodged behind one of the square, featureless buildings and then began to creep closer up the hill.

The figure was probably unaware that he could be seen so easily from below. He was gesturing angrily as he watched Bladrak's men helping the wretched slaves aboard their ships.

I heard a voice.

I could not make out the words, but the tone was more than familiar to me.

I crept closer, anxious to have confirmed by my eyes what had already been confirmed by my ears.

I saw the face now.

It was Bishop Belphig, of course. Every suspicion I had had about him was proved right.

'Have you no understanding?' he was crying. 'That pirate Bladrak will not only make off with most of your labour force—he will turn half of those into soldiers to fight against you.'

I heard a murmured reply, then a group of Silver Warriors came running down the hill, saw me—and charged with their halberds.

I turned and fled, just as Bladrak's boat was leaving.

'We thought we had lost you, Sir Champion,' he grinned. 'What were you doing up there?'

'I was listening to a conversation.'

Halberds fell into the water on either side of us but we were soon out of range.

Bladrak said: 'It will take them time to bring up their heavier weapons. We did well. Not a man wounded, even—and a satisfactory cargo.' He gestured towards the boats crammed with rescued slaves. Then what I had said registered with him.

'Conversation? What did you learn?'

'I learned that Rowenarc has a leader who would bring about her ruin,' I said.

'Belphig?'

'Aye. He's up there, doubtless with the leader of the Silver Warriors on the island. Now I know his main reason for his "hunt". He wished to rid himself of me, for fear I should aid you against his allies—and he needed to make a secret rendezvous with the Silver Warriors.'

Bladrak shrugged. 'I always suspected him of something of the sort. They have no values those folk in Rowernarc.'

'Save, perhaps, their Lord Temporal—Shanosfane. And no human being deserves the fate of these wretches.' I jerked my thumb at the thin, dirty bodies of the Silver Warriors' ex-slaves.

'What would you do about it, Count Urlik?'

'I must think, Sir Bladrak.'

He gave me a long, hard look and said softly: 'Are you sure it is not yet time to use your sword?'

I avoided his eye and stared out to sea. 'I have not said I intend to use the sword at any time.'

'Then I do not think we shall live long,' he said.

CHAPTER FOUR

THE LADY OF THE CHALICE

And thus we came back to the Scarlet Fjord. The freed slaves looked around them in wonder as our boats tied up at quays bathed in rosy light from the honeycombed cliff on the far side of the fjord.

'Best mount extra guards from now on,' Bladrak told one of his lieutenants. Absently, he twisted one of the golden bracelets on his arm. 'Belphig knows us and he knows the Scarlet Fjord. They'll try reprisals.'

Weary from our expedition we went inside and pleasant women brought us meat and wine. There was plenty of extra room in the city of the Scarlet Fjord and the freed slaves would find themselves well provided for. Bladrak was frowning, though, as he sat opposite me and looked across the quartz table.

'Are you still thinking of the Black Sword?' I asked him.

He shook his head. 'No. That's for you to think about. I was considering the implications of Belphig's perfidy. From time to time we have the odd man or woman in the Scarlet Fjord who decided that Rowernarc offers pursuits more to their taste. We allow them to leave, of course, and—they go . . .'

'You mean that Belphig may be aware of many of your plans?' I said.

'You mentioned that he was unnerved by the sound of Urlik's Bell. Plainly he knows everything about you, about the Lady of the Chalice and so on. Equally plainly, he sought to soften you up in Rowernarc—in the hope he could bring you over to his side. When that failed . . .'

'He marooned me. But now he must know I sail with you.'

'Aye. And he will pass on all his information to his alien masters. What do you think they will do then?'

'They will try to strike before we grow any stronger.'

'Aye. But will they strike at the Scarlet Fjord first—or will they take Rowernarc and the cities further up the coast?'

'It will be easier for them to take the cities, I suspect,' I replied. 'Then they can concentrate their full power upon the Scarlet Fjord.'

'That's my guess, also.'

'The question now is—do we remain here, building up our strength for a siege, or do we go to the aid of Rowernarc and the rest?'

'It's a difficult problem.' Bladrak stood up, running his fingers through his red hair. 'I would like to consult one who could offer us wisdom on the matter.'

'You have philosophers here? Or strategists?'

'Not exactly. We have the Lady of the Chalice.'

'She dwells in the Scarlet Fjord? I did not realise . . .'

He smiled and shook his head. 'She may come to the Scarlet Fjord, however.'

'I should like to meet this woman. After all, she seems responsible for my fate.'

'Then come with me,' Bladrak said, and he led me through an inner door and into a long passage which sloped sharply downward.

Soon a strong saline smell reached my nostrils and I noticed that the walls were damp. I guessed that we were actually under the fjord itself.

The passage widened into a chamber. From the roof grew long stalactites in milky blues, yellows and greens. A soft radiance issued from the stalactites themselves and cast our gigantic shadows on the rough igneous rock of the cavern's walls. In the centre of the chamber an area of basalt had been smoothed and levelled and into it had been placed a small staff of about half a man's height. The staff was a deep, lustreless black with mottlings of dark blue. The cavern contained no other artifact.

'What is the staff for?' I asked.

Bladrak shook his head. 'I do not know. It has always been here. It was here long before my ancestors came to the Scarlet Fjord.'

'Has it any connection with the Lady of the Chalice?'

'I think it might have, for it is here that she appears to us.' He looked about him, half nervously I thought. 'Lady?'

It was all he said. Then a distant, high-pitched, oscillating whine came from all around us in the air. The stalactites vibrated and I prayed they would not be brought down on our heads by the sound. The short staff imbedded in the basalt seemed to change colour slightly, but that might have been something cast by one of the vibrating stalactites. The whine increased until it began to sound like a human scream and I recognised it with some trepidation. I blinked my eyes. I thought I saw the outline of the huge golden chalice again. I turned to say something to Bladrak and then looked back in astonishment.

A woman stood there. She was wreathed in golden light. Her dress and her hair were of gold and on her hands she wore gloves.

Her face was covered by a golden veil.

Bladrak kneeled. 'Lady, we need your help again.'

'My help?' came a sweet voice. 'When your great hero Urlik has joined you at last?'

'I have no power of prophecy, my lady,' I replied. 'Bladrak believes that you might have.'

'My own powers are limited and I am not permitted to reveal all I see, even then. What do you wish to know, Sir Champion?'

'Let Bladrak tell you.'

Bladrak climbed to his feet. Quickly he outlined the problem. Should we go to the aid of Rowernarc and the other cities? Or should we wait until the Silver Warriors attacked us?

The Lady of the Chalice seemed to deliberate. 'The fewer killed in this struggle the better I shall like it,' she said. 'It would seem to me that the sooner it is over the more folk will be saved.'

Bladrak gestured with his hands. 'But Rowernarc has brought this on herself. Who is to say how many warriors are on Belphig's side? Perhaps the city will fall without bloodshed...'

'There would be bloodshed soon enough,' said the Lady of the Chalice. 'Belphig would destroy all he did not trust.'

'Likely, aye...' mused Bladrak Morningspear. He glanced at me.

'Is there a way of killing the Silver Warriors?' I asked the mysterious woman. 'At the moment we are badly handicapped.'

'They cannot be killed,' she said. 'Not by your weapons, at least.'

Bladrak shrugged. 'Then I will risk many men in trying to save the worthless citizens of Rowernarc. I am not sure they would like to die for that cause, Lady.'

'Surely some are not worthless,' said she. 'What of Lord Shanosfane? He would be in great danger if Belphig gained complete power over Rowernarc.'

I admitted that Shanosfane was in danger and I agreed that the strange, abstracted Lord Temporal was worth saving from Belphig.

Then she asked, rather strangely: 'Would you say that Lord Shanosfane was a good man?'

'Aye,' I replied. 'Eminently good.'

'I think, then, that you will need him in the near future,' she said.

'Perhaps we can get to Rowernarc before Belphig finishes his business on Nalanarc?' I suggested. 'We could get the populace away before the Silver Warriors attacked.'

'Belphig's business on Nalanarc was finished for him,' Bladrak pointed out. 'And now that he knows he is allied to the Silver Warriors, he will waste no time in attacking.'

'True.'

'But only the Black Sword will defeat Belphig,' said the veiled woman, 'and now you possess it, Lord Urlik.'

'I will not use it,' I said.

'You will use it.' The air pulsed. She vanished.

I recognised the statement. It had no threat in it, only certainty. I had heard it before while marooned on the sea-stag's island.

I rubbed my face with my hands. 'I would be grateful if I was allowed to work out my own destiny for once,' I said. 'For good or ill.'

'Come,' Bladrak began to leave the cavern.

I followed him, lost in my own thoughts. Everything was conspiring to force me into a pattern of behaviour which all my instincts rejected. But perhaps my instincts were wrong ...

We returned to Bladrak's apartments in time to receive a messenger who had just arrived.

'My lords, the Silver Warriors' fleet has left harbour and is sailing directly south.'

'Bound for——?' Bladrak queried.

'For Rowernarc, I think.'

Bladrak snorted. 'We've been wasting time, I see. We'll never reach Rowernarc before they do. Also it could be a trick to divert us. For all I know their real ambition is to draw us off while another fleet attacks the Scarlet Fjord.' He looked sardonically at me. 'We are still in a quandary, Count Urlik.'

'The Lady of the Chalice seemed to indicate that it would be to our advantage if Shanosfane were saved,' I said. 'We must think of him, at least.'

'Risk a fleet for one man of Rowernarc.' Bladrak laughed. 'No, Sir Champion!'

'Then I must go alone,' I said.

'You'll achieve nothing—save to lose us our Hero.'

'Your Hero, Sir Bladrak,' I pointed out, 'has done precious little for you so far.'

'Your role will be clear soon.'

'It is clear now. I have a great respect for Lord Shanosfane. I cannot bear to think of him being butchered by Belphig.'

'I understand—but you cannot risk so much, Count Urlik.'

'I could afford to,' I said, 'if I had an ally.'

'An ally? I could not desert my folk to embark upon an——'

'I speak not of you, Bladrak. I appreciate that you must stay with your people. I did not mean a human ally.'

He looked at me in astonishment. 'Supernatural? What?'

In me now was a mixture of melancholy and relief. There was but one course open to me. I took it. I at once felt that I was giving in and making a courageous decision.

'The Black Sword,' I said.

Bladrak, too, looked as if he had had a weight removed from

his shoulders. He grinned and clapped me on the back. 'Aye. It would seem a shame not to blood it now that you have it.'

'Bring it to me,' I told him.

CHAPTER FIVE

THE WAKING OF THE SWORD

They brought the ebony case and they laid it on the table carved from quartz while conflicting emotions fought within me until I was so dizzy I could scarcely see the thing.

I put my hands upon the case. It felt warm. There seemed to be a faint pulse coming from within it, like the beating of a heart.

I looked at Bladrak who was staring at me, grim-faced. I took hold of the clasp and tried to raise it.

It was tightly locked.

'It will not open,' I said. I was almost glad. 'I cannot move it. Perhaps, after all, it was not meant . . .'

And then, inside my head, loudly came the chant again:

BLACK SWORD
BLACK SWORD
BLACK SWORD
THE BLACK SWORD IS THE CHAMPION'S SWORD
THE WORD OF THE SWORD IS THE CHAMPION'S
LAW
BLACK SWORD
BLACK SWORD
BLACK SWORD
THE BLADE OF THE SWORD HAS THE BLOOD OF
THE SUN
THE HILT OF THE SWORD AND THE HAND ARE
AS ONE
BLACK SWORD
BLACK SWORD
BLACK SWORD
THE RUNES ON THE SWORD ARE THE WORMS
THAT ARE WISE
THE NAME OF THE SWORD IS THE SAME AS THE
SCYTHE

BLACK SWORD
BLACK SWORD
BLACK SWORD
THE DEATH OF THE SWORD IS THE DEATH OF
ALL LIFE
IF THE BLACK SWORD IS WAKENED IT MUST
TAKE ITS BLACK FIEF
BLACK SWORD
BLACK SWORD
BLACK SWORD

Now I wavered in my resolve at the last phrase. A huge sense of doom pressed upon me. I staggered back, my lips writhing, my whole soul in agony.

'No . . .'

Bladrak leapt forward and supported me.

My voice was strangled. 'Bladrak—you must leave here.'

'Why, Lord Urlik, you seem to need . . .'

'Leave here!'

'But I would help you . . .'

'You will perish if you stay.'

'How do you know that?'

'I am not sure—but I do know it. I speak truly, Bladrak. *Leave—for pity's sake!*'

Bladrak hesitated for another moment and then ran from the room, locking the door behind him.

I was alone with the case that held the Black Sword and the voice continued to chant in my head

BLACK SWORD
BLACK SWORD
BLACK SWORD
AROUSE THE BLACK BLADE AND THE PATTERN
IS MADE
THE DEED WILL BE DONE AND THE PRICE WILL
BE PAID
BLACK SWORD
BLACK SWORD
BLACK SWORD

'Very well!' I screamed. 'I will do it. I will take up the Black Sword again. I will pay the price!'

The chanting ceased.

There was a terrible stillness in the room.

I heard my own breath rasping as my eyes fixed on the case on the table and were held by it.

In a low voice I said at last:

'Come to me, Black Sword. We shall be as one again.'

The lid of the case sprang open. A wild, triumphant howling filled the air—an almost human voice which awakened a thousand memories within me.

I was Elric of Melniboné and I defied the Lords of Chaos with my runesword Stormbringer in my hands and a wild joy in my heart . . .

I was Dorian Hawkmoon and I fought against the Best Lords of the Dark Empire and my sword was called The Sword of the Dawn . . .

I was Roland dying at Roncesvalles with the magic blade Durandana slaying half a hundred Saracens . . .

I was Jeremiah Cornelius and this was no sword now but a needle-gun shooting darts as I was chased through a city by a surging, insane mob . . .

I was Prince Corum in the Scarlet Robe, seeking vengeance at the Court of the Gods . . .

I was Artos the Celt, riding with my burning blade uplifted against the invaders of my kingdom's shores . . .

And I was all of these and more than these and sometimes my weapon was a sword, at others it was a spear, at others a gun . . . But always I bore a weapon that was the Black Sword or a part of that strange blade.

Always a weapon—always the warrior.

I was the Eternal Champion and that was my glory and my doom . . .

And a strange mood of reconciliation came over me then and I was proud of my destiny.

Yet why had I denied it?

I recalled a billowing cloud of brightness. I remembered grief. I remembered sealing the sword in its case and swearing I would not bear it again. I remembered a voice and a prophecy . . .

'In refusing one doom, ye shall know another—a greater . . .'

'No doom can be greater,' I shouted.

Then I was John Daker—unhappy, unfulfilled, before the

voice called across the aeons for him to become Erekosë.

The crime I had committed was in refusing the Black Sword.

But why had I refused it? Why had I tried to rid myself of it?

It seemed to me that that had not been the first time I had tried to part my own destiny from that of the Black Sword ...

'*Why?*' *I murmured.* '*Why?*'

'Why?'

Then from the case a strange, black radiance spilled and I was drawn towards it until I stared down upon that familiar sight.

It was a heavy, black broadsword. Carved into its blade and hilt were runes which I could not read. Its pommel was a sphere of gleaming black metal. It was more than five feet long in its blade and its hilt was more than large enough to accommodate two hands.

My own hands reached involuntarily towards it now.

They touched the hilt and the sword seemed to rise and settle comfortably in my grip, purring as a cat might purr.

I shuddered and yet I was filled with joy.

But now I understood what was meant by the term 'unholy joy'.

With this sword in my hands I ceased to be a man and became a demon.

I laughed. My laughter was gigantic and shook the room. I swung the sword about and it shrieked its wild music. I raised it and I brought it down upon the table of quartz.

The table split completely in twain. Chips of quartz flew everywhere.

'This is the Whole Sword!' I cried. 'This is the Cold Sword! This is the Black Sword and soon it must feed!'

In the recesses of my brain I understood that it was rare for me to hold the actual sword. Usually I had a weapon which drew its power from the Black Sword, which was a manifestation of the Black Sword.

Because I had sought to challenge Destiny, Destiny had taken vengeance. What followed could only be accomplished with the whole power of the Black Sword, but I still did not know what it was to be.

One of Bladrak's girls entered the room through another door. Her face was horrified as she saw me.

'My master sent me to ask if——' She screamed.

The Black Sword twisted in my hand and plunged towards her, almost dragging me with it. It buried itself in her body, passing completely through to the other side. She danced in a dreadful jig of death as, with her remaining life, she sought to drag herself off the blade.

'It is cold—aaah, how it is cold!' she sighed.

And then she died.

The sword was wrenched from her. Blood seemed to increase its dark radiance. It howled again.

'No!' I shouted. 'That should not have been! Only my enemies are to be slain!'

And I thought something like a chuckle escaped the sated sword as Bladrak rushed in to see what had happened, looked at me, looked at the sword, looked at the dead girl and groaned in terror.

He rushed to the case. There was a sheath in there and he flung it at me. 'Sheath the thing, Urlik! Sheath it, I beg you!'

Silently I accepted the sheath. Almost without my raising it the Black Sword slid into the scabbard.

Bladrak looked at the poor, dead woman, at the shattered table.

Then he looked at my face and an expression of anguish covered his features.

'Now I know why you did not wish to wield the blade,' he said softly.

I could not speak. I attached the great scabbard to my belt and the Black Sword hung at my side at an angle.

Then I said: 'You all wished me to arouse the blade and use it. Now, I think, we begin to understand the consequences. The Black Sword must be fed. It will feed on friends if it cannot feed on enemies...'

Bladrak turned his eyes away.

'Is a boat ready?' I asked him.

He nodded.

I left the ruined room of death.

CHAPTER SIX

THE BLACK BLADE'S FIEF

They had given me a boat and a steersman.

The boat was a small one, with high, curving sides, plated with red gold and bronze. The steersman sat in front of me, controlling the leather-winged herons which flew low through the twilight air.

The Scarlet Fjord was soon no more than a glow hanging above the distant cliffs, then that vanished and brown cloud enclosed our gloomy world.

For a long while we sped over the black and sluggish sea until the jagged obsidian cliffs came in sight. Then we saw the bay overlooked by Rowernarc—and in the bay were crammed the besieging ships of the Silver Warriors.

Belphig had not wasted time. It was possible that I had arrived too late.

The craft of the invaders were very large and similar in design to Belphig's sea-chariot, but apparently with no *slevahs* to tow them.

We stayed out of sight and the steersman brought the boat to a halt on the crystalline beach quite close to the spot where Belphig's men had first encountered me.

Telling the steersman to await my return, I began to move cautiously along the shore in the direction of the Obsidian City.

Keeping to the cover of the rocks, I was able to round the corner of the bay and see exactly what I faced.

Plainly Rowernarc had capitulated without a battle. Prisoners were being herded down the ramps towards the ships.

Handling their halberds as awkwardly as ever, the slim Silver Warriors were dotted everywhere on the causeways.

Belphig himself was not in sight, but half-way up the cliff I saw my chariot, its bears in their harness, being trundled down to the beach. Doubtless this was part of their booty.

Shanosfane was not among the prisoners. I guessed that Belphig had had him confined to his 'province' of Dhötgard for the moment—if the Lord Spiritual had not already killed the Lord Temporal.

But how was I to reach Dhötgard when every level was crowded with the alien invaders?

Even with the aid of the Black Sword I would surely be swamped by weight of numbers if I tried to cut my way up to Dhötgard. And if I reached the place, how would I return?

Then a thought came to me as I watched my bears being urged towards the sea where a series of planks had been placed between the shallows and the nearest ship.

Deliberating no further I leapt up, drew my sword and ran for the chariot.

I had almost reached it before I was seen. A Silver Warrior shouted in a high, fluting voice, flinging his halberd at me. I knocked it aside with the sword, which, for all its weight, handled as easily as a fencing foil. I sprang into the chariot and gathered up the reins, turning the bears back towards the Obsidian City.

'Ho, Render! Ho, Growler!'

As if their spirits had risen at my sudden appearance, the bears reared in their harness and wheeled about.

'Ho, Longclaw! Ho, Snarler!'

The wheels of the chariot scraped round in the crystal rock and then we were driving straight for the causeway.

I ducked as more halberds were thrown, but they were poor throwing weapons at the best of times and the Silver Warriors' lack of skill with them did not help. Slaves and soldiers scattered and we had reached the first level in no time.

Now the Black Sword was crooning again. An evil song, a mocking song.

As I raced past them, I slashed at warriors who tried to stick me with their weapons and now when I struck their armour it was they who yelled, not me . . .

Up and up we charged and I felt an old, familiar battle-joy returning. The Black Sword cut off heads and limbs and bright blood streamed the length of its blade, dappling the sides of the chariots and the white pelts of the bears.

'On, Render! On, Longclaw!'

We were almost at the level of Dhötgard. Everywhere men were shouting and running in all directions.

'On, Snarler! On, Growler!'

Even faster ran my mighty bears until we came to the great door which protected Dhötgard. It had been drawn right back. I guessed that some spy in Shanosfane's household had been paid to do this. But it suited me now for I was able to drive the chariot right into the place and continue at breakneck speed through the very passages themselves.

At last I reached the plain chamber where I had first met Shanosfane. I brushed aside the curtain and there he was.

He looked a little thinner, there was some hurt in his eyes, but he looked up from a manuscript as if he had been disturbed only for a moment when the Silver Warriors had arrived in Rowernarc.

'My Lord Urlik?'

'I have come to rescue you, Lord Shanosfane.'

His black features showed mild surprise.

'Belphig will kill you now that he has helped betray Rowernarc.'

'Why should Belphig kill me?'

'You threaten his rule.'

'Rule?'

'Lord Shanosfane, if you remain here you are doomed. There will be no more reading. No more study.'

'I do it only to pass the time...'

'Do you not fear death?'

'No.'

'Well, then...' I sheathed my sword, ran forward and knocked him sharply on the back of the neck. He slumped on to the desk. I flung him over my shoulder and ran for the exit. My bears were snarling as Silver Warriors rushed towards us. I dumped Shanosfane in the chariot and leapt at the warriors.

Plainly they were used to weapons that could not harm them. The Black Sword whined and howled and it sheered through their strange armour to reveal that they were, indeed, very much like men. Their blood spilled as easily. Their innards spewed from the cuts the blade made. Their silver-flecked faces showed their pain.

I got back into the chariot, flicked the reins, turning it in the narrow passage and then gathering speed as we made for the main door.

Then I saw Belphig. He yelped as he saw our headlong approach and he flattened himself against the wall. I leaned out, trying to reach him with the sword, but he was too far distant.

We went around the door block and out on to the causeway again, going down much faster than we had come up.

This time our path was not blocked by Silver Warriors. They had learned to be wary. But they still flung their halberds at a safe distance and two nicked slight wounds in my left arm and my right cheek.

I was laughing at them again, holding my huge sword aloft. More powerful than the sword of Erekosë (which had been one of its partial manifestations, perhaps) it thrummed out its evil song of death as my bears bore us towards the beach.

There was cheering now, from some quarters, as the prisoners saw me re-emerge. I shouted to them.

'Fight, men of Rowernarc! Fight! Turn on the Silver Warriors! Slay them if you can!'

Downward the chariot rumbled.

'Kill them or you will die!'

Some of the prisoners picked up halberds and began to fling them at their vanquishers. The Silver Warriors were again startled, not knowing how to react.

'Now flee!' I cried. 'Make for the depths of the mountains and then head along the coast for the Scarlet Fjord. You will be welcome there—and safe. The Black Sword will defend you!'

I hardly knew what I was shouting, but it had a surprising effect on the spiritless people of Rowernarc. While the Silver Warriors were confused, they began to run. They still had time to be soldiers, I thought. And soldiers the survivors would become—for now they knew what their fate would be if they did not fight.

Laughing in my crazy battle-joy I drove the chariot down the cliff and its wheels bounced over the crystal.

'Shanosfane is safe!' I called to those who listened. 'Your leader is with me.' As best I could I raised his prone body. 'He is alive but unconscious!' I saw one of his eyelids flutter. He would not be unconscious for long.

Belphig and a party of Silver Warriors were still in pursuit. From one of the entrances now came Morgeg and his men on their seal-beasts and I knew I had to fear these more than the clumsy aliens.

Across the beach they crashed in pursuit. A spear grazed the shoulder of one of my bears. The powerful animals were labouring somewhat now, for I had driven them hard.

And then, half-way to where I had left the boat, the chariot wheel hit a rock and Shanosfane and I were flung on to the ground as the bears raced on, dragging the chariot behind them. It bounced, hit another rock, righted itself and, riderless, disappeared into the gloom.

I put Shanosfane over my shoulder again and began to run, but the thump of the seal-beasts' fins came close behind. I saw the boat ahead. I turned to look at Morgeg and the others. They would reach me before I could get to the boat.

Shanosfane was moaning, rubbing his head. I put him down. 'See that boat, Lord Shanosfane. It will take you to safety. Get to it as quickly as you can.'

I took the Black Sword in both hands as the dazed Shanosfane staggered away.

Then I prepared to stand my ground.

Morgeg and six other riders, all armed with axes, charged at me. I whirled the huge sword around my head and sheered half through the necks of two of the seals. They bellowed as the blood pumped from their veins. They tried to come on, but collapsed and threw their riders from their saddles. I killed one of the riders at once, plunging the Black Sword through steel and padding straight into his heart. I brought the blade round and killed a man who was still mounted. He jerked in his saddle and then toppled out.

The other man on foot came at me crablike with his battle-axe circling his head. I chopped at the haft of the axe and the blade went spinning through the air to strike a rider directly in the face and knock him from his saddle. I drove my sword through the weaponless warrior's gorget.

Now Morgeg fought to control his frightened mount. He glared at me in hatred.

'You are tenacious, Count Urlik,' he said.

'It seems so.' I feinted at him.

There was only one rider left alive save Morgeg. I lowered my sword and spoke to the man. 'Would you leave while I kill Morgeg? Or will you stay and be slain with him.'

The man's pale face twitched, his mouth dropped open, he tried to say something, failed and wheeled his seal-beast about, heading back to Rowernarc.

Morgeg said quietly 'I think I should like to return, also.'

'You cannot,' I said simply. 'I have to repay you for marooning me on that island.'

'I thought you were dead.'

'You did not check.'

'I thought the sea-stag killed you.'

'I killed the sea-stag.'

He licked his lips. 'In that case, I should definitely like to return to Rowernarc.'

I lowered the Black Sword. 'You may do so if you tell me one thing. Who leads you?'

'Why, Belphig leads us!'

'No. I mean who is the leader of the Silver Warr——'

Morgeg thought he had seen a chance. He swung his axe down on me.

But I blocked the blow with the flat of the sword. I turned my own weapon and the axe flew from his hand. The sword could not be stopped as it went to his groin and the point drove deeply in.

'Cold...' murmured Morgeg as his eyes closed. 'So cold...'

The corpse fell backwards in the saddle and the seal-beast reared and turned, charging towards the bay.

I saw Belphig at the head of a group of Silver Warriors. There were a score of them and I wondered if even the Black Sword could deal with so many.

I heard a shout from seaward. I heard the noise of wings beating overhead.

'Lord Urlik! Now!'

It was the steersman's voice. He had bundled Shanosfane aboard and had come along the coast to find me.

I sheathed the Black Sword and plunged knee-deep into the water. The stuff clung to my legs, hampering me. Belphig and his men were almost upon us. Behind him, in the way, everything was still in confusion.

I grasped the smooth side of the boat and hauled myself in, gasping. Immediately the steersman turned the herons and we were heading out to sea.

Belphig and the Silver Warriors came to a stop at the edge of the water and were soon swallowed in the gloom.

We raced back for the Scarlet Fjord.

Bladrak Morningspear had an unusually grim expression on his face as he sat in an amber chair and looked across the room at Shanosfane and myself.

We were in another room of his apartments, as far away from the chamber of death as possible. I had taken off the scabbarded Black Sword and leaned the thing against the wall.

'Well,' said Bladrak quietly, 'the Black Sword has earned its price it seems. You must have killed many Silver Warriors as well as those riders of Belphig's—and perhaps you showed the folk of Rowernarc that there was some point in defending themselves.'

I nodded.

'And you, my Lord Shanosfane, are you pleased that you have avoided death?'

Bladrak spoke almost sardonically.

Shanosfane looked at him from those deep, detached eyes. 'I am not sure what difference there is between life and death, Sir Bladrak.'

Bladrak's expression seemed to indicate that he had made a point. He got up and began to pace about.

I said to Shanosfane: 'Do you know who rules the Silver Warriors?'

Shanosfane looked slightly surprised. 'Why, Belphig, of course ...'

'He means that he wants to know who commands Belphig,' Bladrak said. 'Who is supreme ruler of the Silver Warriors?'

'Why, Belphig. Bishop Belphig. He is their supreme ruler.'

'But he is not of their race!' I exclaimed.

'He has their queen prisoner.' Shanosfane's gaze wandered around the room and then fixed curiously on the Black Sword. 'They are not really warriors, those people. They are peaceful. They have never known war. But Belphig makes them do his will—for if they do not, he will destroy their queen, whom they love above life.'

I was astonished and I could see that Bladrak was equally surprised. 'So that is why they are such poor halberdiers,' I murmured.

'They know how to build engines to make ships move through the water,' Shanosfane said. 'They have several such mechanical skills. Belphig told me all this.'

'But why is he enslaving our people?' Bladrak demanded. 'What use is there in it?'

Shanosfane looked calmly at Bladrak. 'I do not know. What use is there in any activity? Perhaps Belphig's plan is as good as any other.'

'You have no idea of his ultimate ambitions?' I said.

'I told you. None at all. I did not think to enquire.'

'Do you not care that your people are being enslaved— killed!' Bladrak shouted. 'Does not that touch you anywhere in that cold soul of yours?'

'They were slaves already,' Shanosfane said reasonably. 'And they were dying. How much longer do you think our race could have lived like that?'

Bladrak turned his back on the Lord Temporal.

'Lord Urlik, you wasted your time,' he said.

'Because Lord Shanosfane does not think as we do,' I replied, 'it does not follow that he was not worth saving.'

'I was not worth saving.' A peculiar look came into Shanosfane's eyes. 'I do not think I have been saved. Who told you to rescue me?'

'We decided to do it ourselves,' I replied. And then I paused. 'No, perhaps not—perhaps it was the Lady of the Chalice who suggested it.'

Shanosfane returned his attention to the Black Sword.

'I think I would like it if you could leave me alone,' he said. 'I would meditate.'

Bladrak and I went to the door and walked out into the corridor.

'Well, perhaps he was worth saving after all,' Bladrak admitted reluctantly. 'He gave us information we should not have had otherwise. But I have no liking for the fellow and cannot see why you admire him. He is nothing but a——'

We stopped in our tracks as a blood-curdling scream came from the room we had just left. We looked at each other, sharing a certain knowledge.

We ran back towards the door.

But the Black Sword had done its work. Shanosfane lay spread-eagled on the floor with the blade waving from the middle of his chest like an obscene plant. Whether the sword had attacked him or whether he had managed to kill himself with it we would never know.

Shanosfane was not dead. His lips were moving.

I bent to listen to the words he whispered. 'I had not realised it would be so—so chill ...'

Those incredibly intelligent eyes closed and he spoke no more.

I tugged the Black Sword from his body and put it back in its sheath.

Bladrak was pale. 'Was that why the Lady of the Chalice made you bring him here?' he said.

I did not understand him at first. 'What do you mean?'

'Did the sword need the life of a good man—an especially good man—as its price for helping us? The Black Sword's reward—the soul of the Black King?'

I remembered the words of the chant:

If the Black Sword is wakened, it must take its Black Fief ...

105

I clenched my hands together as I looked down at the corpse of the scholar king.

'Oh, Bladrak,' I said, 'I am afraid of our future.'

And a coldness, colder than the coldest ice, filled the room.

BOOK FOUR

The Blood of the Sun

A knife, a cup and a man shall be
The means by which the world's set free.
                    —The Chronicle of the Black Sword

CHAPTER ONE

SIEGE OF THE SCARLET FJORD

Depression settled over us and even the fires of the Scarlet Fjord seemed to fade.

We lived in the shadow of the Black Sword and now I had an inkling of the reasons why I had wanted to rid myself of it.

One could not master the sword. It demanded lives as some greedy Moloch—some fierce, barbaric god of ancient times—demanded sacrifice. And, what was worse, it often chose its own sacrifices from among the friends of the man who bore it.

A jealous sword, indeed.

I know that Bladrak did not blame me for what had taken place. In fact he claimed that the fault was shared between himself and the Lady of the Chalice—for they had encouraged me, against my will, to awaken the Black Sword and use it.

'It has already aided us,' I pointed out. 'Without it, I should not have survived in Rowernarc and we should not have learned from Shanosfane the truth of Belphig's status and the nature of his hold over the Silver Warriors.'

'It has been well paid for its work . . .' Bladrak growled.

'If we knew were Belphig hid this queen,' I said, 'then we could free her. The Silver Warriors would refuse to serve Belphig and the threat would be over.'

'But we know not where, in the whole world, she is!'

'If the Lady of the Chalice were to be asked . . .' I began, but Bladrak silenced me.

107

'I am not sure that the Lady works entirely in our interest,' he said. 'I think she uses us in some larger scheme of her own.'

'Aye—you could be right.'

Now we walked along the quays, staring down at the red-stained water, at the many boats we were preparing for our war against the Silver Warriors. The knowledge that the slender, awkward aliens fought us only because they had been forced to do so by Belphig took some of the savagery out of our feelings and our work had slowed accordingly.

Unable to hate the Silver Warriors, it was harder for us to contemplate killing them. But we should have to kill them or see the whole of humanity slain or enslaved.

I looked across the fjord to the mysterious source of its heat and light—the honeycomb cliff from which the scarlet radiance issued.

There was a power there but I could not begin to guess at its nature. Something created millenia before which continued to burn at the same constant temperature while the rest of the world grew cold. Once, I thought, the Scarlet Fjord had been something other than a camp for the outlaws who chose not to live in the soft decadence of cities like Rowernarc. Was the Lady of the Chalice the last descendant of the scientists who had dwelt here? Perhaps Shanosfane could have told us. Perhaps that was why the Black Sword had killed him, because we were meant to remain in ignorance . . .

Suddenly Bladrak put a hand on my shoulder. He cocked his head and listened.

I heard it then. The sound of a horn. It blew louder.

'The guards,' said Bladrak. 'Come, Lord Urlik, let's see why they sound the alarm.' He leapt into a boat which had already been harnessed to a pair of the heron-like flying creatures. They were asleep on the perches built along the quayside. He shook their reins and awakened them as I joined him. The birds squawked and took to the air. We headed towards the narrow opening of the fjord.

Between the tall, black cliffs we moved until the open sea was in sight. And then we saw the reason for the guards' alarum.

It was Belphig's fleet.

There were between five hundred and a thousand great ships massing there and the air was full of the drone of their engines. Low, sluggish waves rocked our craft as their wash reached us.

'Belphig brings all his strength against us!' Bladrak rasped. 'Our boats could never hope to beat those huge craft...'

'But in one thing their size is against them,' I pointed out. 'They can only enter the fjord one at a time. If we mass our warriors on the cliffs above the opening, we might be able to attack them when they try to enter the approach to the Scarlet Fjord.'

He brightened a little. 'Aye. It might work. Let's get back.'

We were waiting in the heights when the first of the great craft, with its strange pyramidal arrangement of decks, nosed its way between the cliffs. We had arranged boulders on the ledges in readiness.

The ship came directly beneath us and I drew the Black Sword and shouted: 'Now!'

The boulders were levered over the ledges and crashed into the decks. Several crunched straight through, while others smashed down the terraces, taking timbers and warriors with them.

A mighty cheer went up from the warriors of the Scarlet Fjord as the ship keeled over and the soldiers in their silver armour were toppled into the viscous sea which sucked them down as they struggled and screamed in their strange high-pitched voices.

As I watched them die, I thought that these poor creatures were as much victims of Belphig's perfidy as were we. Yet what else could we do but kill them? They fought so that a queen they loved more than life would not perish. We fought for our freedom. What Belphig himself fought for I was yet to learn.

Another ship tried to enter the gulf and again we showered down our boulders. This ship split in twain, both ends rising steepily out of the water like the slowly closing snout of some sea monster, sandwiching those who had survived and crushing them before there was a burst of white hotness from the centre and the waters bubbled and steam struck our faces. I realised that we had destroyed one of the engines. They seemed unstable things. Perhaps we had found another weakness of the Silver Warriors.

After two more attempts, the ships withdrew, surrounding the entrance to the fjord in a semicircle many craft deep.

The siege of the Scarlet Fjord had begun in earnest.

Bladrak and I conferred in his apartments again. His spirits had lifted with our victories but now, as the implications dawned on him, he began to frown.

'You are afraid that we cannot sustain a long siege,' I said.

He nodded. 'We grow much of what we need in our cavern gardens, but the slaves we have rescued have tripled our numbers and the gardens cannot support so many. Our raids brought us the extra food we needed, but with Belphig's ships blocking the fjord we can do no more raiding.'

'How long do you think we can last?'

He shrugged his shoulders. 'Twenty days or so. We have no stores. They all went to feed the newcomers. Crops continue to grow, but not fast enough. Belphig probably knows this.'

'I am sure he does and is counting on it.'

'What are we to do, Lord Urlik? Go and do battle? At least we will die swiftly . . .'

'That is the last resort. Is there no other way out of the fjord?'

'Not by sea. And the path across the mountains leads only to the ice wastes. We should perish there as quickly as we'd perish here.'

'How long does it take to reach the ice?'

'On foot? Eight days, I think. I have never made the journey.'

'So even if a foraging party was sent out it could not expect to find food and return in time.'

'Exactly.'

I rubbed at my beard, thinking deeply. Eventually I said: 'Then there is only one thing to do at this point.'

'What is that?'

'We must seek the advice of the Lady of the Chalice. Whatever her motives, she seems to want Belphig defeated. She must aid us, if she can.'

'Very well,' said Bladrak. 'Let us go now to the cavern where the dark staff is.'

'Lady?'

Bladrak looked around him, his face shadowed in the soft, weird glow from the stalactites.

The strong smell of salt was in my nostrils. While Bladrak called the Lady of the Chalice, I inspected the short staff that was imbedded in the basalt of the floor. I touched it and withdrew my fingers with a gasp, for it had burned them. Then I realised that it was not extreme heat that had caused the pain—

but extreme cold.

'Lady?'

The thin whine came and it grew to an oscillating shriek. I turned, caught a glimpse of an outline of a great chalice, saw it fade as the shriek died, and then the Lady of the Chalice, clad in golden radiance, her face, as before, completely veiled, stood before us.

'Belphig has almost vanquished you,' she said. 'You should have used the Black Sword sooner.'

'And slain more friends?' I asked.

'You are too sentimental for a great Champion,' she said. 'The issues for which you fight are vast in scope and implication.'

'I am tired of great issues, madam.'

'Then why did Bladrak summon me?'

'Because there was nothing else to do. We are boxed up and will eventually die. The only solution I can see is to rescue the Queen of the Silver Warriors whom Belphig has captured. If she is freed, then Belphig will lose his main strength.'

'That is true.'

'But we know not where to seek this queen,' Bladrak said.

'Ask me a direct question,' the Lady of the Chalice told him.

'Where is the Queen of the Silver Warriors?' I asked. 'Do you know?'

'Aye—I know. She is at Moon, a thousand miles from here across the ice. She is guarded both by Belphig's men and by enchantments of Belphig's arrangement. She cannot leave her apartments and neither can she be visited, save by Belphig himself.'

'So she cannot be rescued.'

'She can be by one man—by you, Urlik, with the aid of the Black Sword.'

I looked at her sharply. 'This is why you helped Bladrak summon me. This is why you brought the sword here and made me use it. For reasons of your own you wish the Silver Queen freed.'

'A simple judgement, Count Urlik. But it will benefit us all if she is freed, I agree.'

'I could not cross a thousand miles of ice on foot. Even if I had not lost my bear chariot, I would not be able to get there in time to free the queen and save the Scarlet Fjord.'

'There is one way,' said the Lady of the Chalice. 'A dangerous way.'

'By using a boat as a sled and having the herons drag it?' I said. 'They would not last that long and I suspect that the boats are not sturdy enough to——'

'I do not mean that.'

'Then explain quickly, Lady,' I said grimly.

'The people who created the Scarlet Fjord were engineers who experimented with many devices. Many were unsuccessful. Many were partially successful. When they went away from here having found a means of travelling through time, they left some of their inventions behind them. One of these was sealed in a cave in a mountain on the far side of this range, near the ice wastes. It was an air chariot, flying under its own power, but it was abandoned because of one defect. The engine used radiated a substance which enfeebled the pilot, blinded him and eventually killed him.'

'And you want me to use such a craft to go to Moon?' I laughed. 'And die before I reach the place? What would be accomplished by that?'

'Nothing. I do not know how long the radiation takes to kill. It could be that you would get to Moon before that happened.'

'Are there any permanent effects of these rays?'

'None that I know of.'

'Where exactly is this craft hidden?'

'There is a pass that leads through the mountains to the ice. At the end of the pass is a mountain that stands alone. Steps are carved into the mountain and at the top of the steps is a sealed door. You must break the door and enter. There you will find the air chariot.'

I frowned. I still distrusted the Lady of the Chalice. She, after all, had been the immediate cause of my separation from Ermizhad and my subsequent agony of mind.

'I will do this thing, Lady,' I said, 'if you will promise me something.'

'What is that?'

'That you will reveal all that you know of my fate and my place in this universe.'

'If you are successful I promise I shall tell you all I know.'

'Then I leave at once for Moon.'

CHAPTER TWO

THE CITY CALLED MOON

And so I left the Scarlet Fjord, climbing up into the black, igneous cliffs that brooded eternally beneath the dark, twilight sky. I had a map with me, some provisions and my sword. My bulky furs keeping out the worst of the cold, I moved through the mountains as rapidly as was possible.

I slept little, with the result that I could barely keep my eyes open and the whorls of obsidian, the frozen cascades of basalt, the oddly shaped pumice visible in all directions took on the appearance of leering faces, of menacing figures of giants and monsters, until I felt surrounded by the creatures of nightmare and I gripped my sword tighter but continued, doggedly, to move on. And at last I saw the ice plains ahead and the clouds thinned out to reveal the red sphere of the sun, the faint stars gleaming behind it.

I welcomed that sight. If I had thought the ice gloomy and bleak when I first found myself in this world, it had been nothing compared with the mood of the mountains which surrounded Earth's last, dark sea. I trudged over the smooth, glassy rock of the pass and I saw the mountain ahead of me.

As the Lady of the Chalice had said, it stood alone, directly before me, on the edge of the ice plain.

I staggered as sleep tried to overcome me. I forced my feet to plod the last half-mile to the base of the mountain where ancient steps had been carved. And on the first of those steps I succumbed to sleep, not knowing for what new task my energies would be needed.

I awoke only barely refreshed and began to climb the steps until I came at length to what had evidently once been the mouth of a natural cave. But that cave mouth had been sealed with molten rock. The length and breadth was filled with a flow of red and yellow obsidian.

I had expected to find a door which I should be able to force, but there was no means of opening this!

I turned and looked back over the mountains. The brown clouds clung to them, increasing their enigmatic appearance. They seemed to share the joke which the Lady of the Chalice had played upon me.

'Damn you!' I yelled.

'Damn you,' they replied. 'Damn you.' And those echoes damned me a hundred times before they died.

Snarling with frustrated anger I drew the Black Sword. Its black radiance spilled out against the obsidian flow. Fiercely I attacked that which sealed the cavern's entrance. The blade bit deep into the rock and pieces of it flew in all directions.

Astonished, I struck again. And again a huge piece of the glassy stone fell away as if blasted.

Again the Black Sword crashed against the rock. And this time, with a rumble, it collapsed completely, revealing a dark chamber. I stepped over the rubble, sheathing the sword. I peered about me, but could see nothing. From my belt I took the torch Bladrak had given me just before I left. I depressed the stud in the handle and a faint light blossomed.

There was the machine the Lady of the Chalice had told me I should find . . .

But she had not told me I should also find the pilot.

He sat in the air chariot and he stared at me in silence, grinning as if in anticipation of my fate. He was long and thin and dressed in the silver armour of those who now served Belphig. He lounged awkwardly in the seat and I guessed he had lounged in the same attitude for centuries, for it was a fleshless skull that grinned at me and fleshless hands that gripped the side of the chariot. I guessed that he had been left there as a warning, perhaps, of the lethal rays of the chariot's engine. With an oath I knocked the skull from the neck and dragged the bones out of the car, hurling them across the cavern floor.

The Lady of the Chalice had told me that I should find the controls simple enough. She had been right. There were no instruments as such that I recognised, merely a crystal rod rising from the floor. By squeezing the rod in my hand I could activate the engine. By pushing the rod forward I could move ahead, by pushing it back I could slow my speed and stop, by pulling it back at an angle I could gain height and by pushing it forward at an angle I could lose height. Similarly the crystal rod could be moved from side to side.

I was anxious to leave the former pilot behind. I got into the chariot and squeezed the rod. Immediately the whole chariot began to glow with a pink luminosity so that it resembled flesh. A throb came from below my feet and I guessed that the engine was there. I licked my dry lips and pushed the lever very slightly forward. The air chariot began to move towards the entrance of the cave. I took it into the air a few feet to avoid the rubble and then we were in the open air again and I discovered that quite small movements of my hand would control the craft. I inspected my map and took a bearing from the compass imbedded in the top of the lever, then I increased speed and headed for the city called Moon.

The obsidian mountains had disappeared and now there was only ice—seemingly infinite ice that streamed past me as I flew. Occasionally the flat plain was broken by frozen drifts and spires but for the most part nothing relieved that cold, desolate landscape.

I began to doubt that the Lady of the Chalice had been right when she had mentiond the engine's poisonous radiations, but soon I realised that my vision had dimmed slightly, that I felt lethargic and my bones ached.

I was driving the air chariot at its maximum speed, but there was no clear means of judging how fast that was. The cold air bit at my flesh and frost rimed my beard and my thick coat was blown about as the white breath was whipped from my mouth.

The discomfort increased. It also seemed to me that I was leaving the sun far behind, that the world was growing darker.

Soon the sun was close to the horizon and the stars blazed more brightly in the sky. But by this time I had fallen back against the support of my seat and nausea shook my body.

I was dying, I was sure. At one stage I was forced to slow my speed and vomit over the side of the craft. I wanted to stop altogether, to get away from the source of my discomfort, but I knew that to leave the aircraft would be to ensure my death. I increased speed again.

And then I saw it ahead. It was a huge white mountain, pitted with great craters, rising out of the ice. I recognised it, of course, for it was the moon itself. How many thousands of years had passed since it had crashed into the Earth? A dim memory came back to me. I was sure I had witnessed this sight before. A name, an impression of despair. What was the name?

It had gone.

With the last of my strength I brought the air chariot to a skidding halt on the ice and pulled my aching body from it.

Then I began to crawl across the ice towards the towering mountain that had once been Earth's satellite.

The farther from the air chariot I crawled the more my strength began to return. By the time I had reached the curved side of the mountain I felt greatly recovered. I could see now that even the mountain was covered with a thin layer of ice in some parts, but not enough to obscure its outlines. Above me I could see a light gleaming and wondered if this was an entrance to the city the Silver Warriors had been forced to desert when they joined Belphig in his war against us. There was nothing for it but to begin to climb. The ice and the rock were rough enough to make climbing fairly easy but I was forced to rest several times and had by no means regained my full strength when I neared the top and saw fierce light suddenly burst out from the centre of a crater and a dozen riders, mounted on seal-beasts, became framed against it.

I had been seen. Perhaps Belphig had even been prepared for my coming.

I slid down the walls of the crater, put my back against the rock, drew out the Black Sword in both hands and awaited the riders.

They charged me with the long, barbed harpoons I had last seen when we had hunted the sea-stag. One of them would rip me from chin to stomach if it pierced my armour.

But the Black Sword itself seemed to be lending me energy. With a single movement I swung it so that I sheared through the head of every harpoon. They clattered to the rock and the useless shafts thudded into the stone as the astonished riders pulled their beasts up short. I plunged the blade into the throat of the nearest seal-beast and it coughed and collapsed, tumbling its rider forward so that I could bring the sword crashing down to shear into his back as he fell.

The laughter began to bubble from my lips now.

I jeered at them as I slew them. They milled in confusion, drawing axes and swords from their scabbards, shouting to each other. An axe struck my mailed shoulder but did not cut through the links. I killed my antagonist with a stroke that cut his face in half and the impetus of my swing clove the body of the man beside him.

They tried to press in, to hamper my movements so that they could cut me down. But the Black Sword would not let them. It moved so rapidly that it opened their ranks every time they managed to close them. A hand, still clutching a sword, flew away into the shadows. A head dropped to the ground. A body spilled entrails over the high saddle. Everywhere the Black

Sword swept it left red ruin in its wake.

And at last they were all dead, save for a few seal-beasts that lumbered back towards the source of the bright light.

I followed them, still laughing.

Instead of exhausting me, the slaughter seemed to have filled me with extra power. I felt light-headed and light-footed, too. I raced after the seal-beasts, blinking in the light, and saw them moving down a long metal ramp which curved into the bowels of the fallen sphere.

More cautiously now I began to move down the ramp. I was just in time, for two doors began to move across the opening and met. I prayed that I had not entered a trap.

Down and down I went until I could see a floor below me. It seemed made of molten silver and it rippled like water, but as I reached it and set a wary foot upon it it felt solid enough.

From out of a doorway in the far wall three more men came running. They, too, were dressed in the bulbous armour of Rowernarc, but they carried the double-bladed halberds I had until now only seen in the hands of the Silver Warriors.

These men were more skilled with the weapons. They spread out and began to swing the things around their heads. I watched them all warily, seeking an opening.

Then one released his and it whistled through the air at me. I flung up my sword to block it and just managed to hurl it aside as the next halberd flew—and then the next. I dodged one and was caught a glancing blow by the other. I was flung to the ground, the Black Sword leaving my hand and skidding across that floor of rippling silver.

Weaponless I rose to my feet as Belphig's men drew their swords. They were grinning. They knew I was doomed.

I looked for the sword but it was too far away to reach in time. I backed away from the warriors and my foot struck something. I glanced down. It was the haft of one of the fallen halberds. They saw it at the same time and began to run towards me. I picked up the halberd, knocked one swordsman in the face with the butt and rammed the spike into another's throat. Then I burst through them and ran for the sword.

But they closed with me before I could reach it. I turned again, blocking a thrust with the shaft and then reversing the movement to bring the axe-blade down on to the helm of the second man. He staggered, dazed, and I skidded across the floor to the sword.

It settled into my hands and it began to moan in my hands

117

like a savage hound that needs to kill.

I let it kill. I split my first assailant from skull to midriff and I chopped the body of the second man in two.

Then I shuddered as the battle-fever began to leave me. Sheathing the sword again I ran towards the entrance through which the warriors had come.

I was in a long, twisting corridor. It was more like a tube, for it was completely round and the floor curved steeply upwards on both sides. Down this I ran and emerged at length into a spherical chamber. I had a feeling that these passages had not originally been used by human beings but had possibly carried traffic or liquids of some kind. Steps led up to the domed roof of the chamber. I climbed them and emerged in a circular room which had a roof like frosted glass. I peered through the glass and realised that it formed the floor of the chamber above me.

But I could see no means of reaching that chamber. Then I thought I saw something move in the room above. I drew my sword.

An opening suddenly appeared in the smooth ceiling. A perfectly round opening in the exact centre of the circle. Then a kind of clear tube descended until it was only a few feet above the floor of the lower chamber. There were handholds on the inside of the tube.

Still wary, I approached the tube and began to climb, the Black Sword balanced in my right hand. I poked my head over the top and there was a sparsely furnished room of great size. Walls and floor were of the same rippling silver. A white bed was there and various chairs and objects whose use I could not guess. And standing near the bed was a woman whose skin was silver, whose eyes were deep black and whose dress was blood red. Her hair was nearly white and her beauty was ethereal. She smiled at me and she moved her lips, but I could not hear her.

I advanced across the transparent floor towards her and suddenly my face struck something cold and hard and I recoiled. I put out my hand and felt smoothness. I was separated from the Silver Queen by an invisible wall.

She gestured, trying to tell me something, but I could not understand her.

What kind of enchantment had Belphig put upon her? His scientific powers were either much greater than he had led me to suspect or else, more likely, he had borrowed them from the Silver Warriors whose ancestors, I now guessed, were the same

118

scientists who had originally occupied the place I knew as the Scarlet Fjord.

Desperation now consumed me. I took the Black Sword and I struck a mighty blow against the invisible wall.

A dreadful shrieking filled the air. A shock ran the length of my body and I was hurled backward. My senses swam. I had grown to rely too much on the power of the Black Sword, I thought, as I collapsed into oblivion.

CHAPTER THREE

THE PHOENIX AND THE QUEEN

There was a chanting in my ears:

BLACK SWORD
BLACK SWORD
BLACK SWORD
THE BLADE OF THE SWORD HAS THE BLOOD OF
THE SUN ...

I opened my eyes and saw the stars in the dark sky. I turned my head, realising that I was in the air chariot again.

At the wheel sat a man in silver armour.

This must be a dream. I was dreaming that the skeleton was piloting the chariot.

If not, then I was a prisoner of the Silver Warriors. I straightened my back and felt the pommel of my sword. I was not tied and I had not been disarmed.

The pilot in silver armour turned his head—and I saw that it was no man at all but the woman I had seen just before I lost consciousness. She had a sardonic look in her black eyes.

'I thank you for your valour in saving me,' she said.

I knew the voice.

'Your sword shattered the barrier. Now we return to the Scarlet Fjord so that I may tell my warriors I am free and they need do Belphig's work no longer.'

'You are the Lady of the Chalice,' I said incredulously.

'That is what Bladrak's people called me.'

'Then all my fighting was in vain. You were already free!'

She smiled. 'No. What you saw was only a manifestation. I

119

could not have appeared anywhere else but in that chamber—
the chamber of the staff. Belphig did not realise that I had a
means of communicating with his enemies.'

'But I saw the chalice at sea!'

'The image of the chalice could be projected to a few other
places, true, but I could not transfer my own image there.'

I looked at her with deep suspicion. 'And how came you by
the Black Sword?'

'The folk of Moon have much wisdom, Sir Champion. We
were great once. There was a prophecy that you would come
again, awakening from your Frozen Keep. It seemed nothing but
a legend, but I studied it for I needed to hope. I discovered a
great deal.'

'And you promised to tell me everything you learned.'

'Aye, I did.'

'First, you could inform me what Belphig's ambition is.'

'Belphig is a fool—though cunning. He knew of Moon and
he found it eventually, having trekked for weeks across the ice
with his men. Having forgotten that war existed, we trusted
him. He learned many of our secrets and then, one day, in-
prisoned me as you found me. He then forced the Silver Warriors to serve him, as you know.'

'But why?'

The Silver Queen swayed in her seat and I realised that the
rays from the craft's engine were affecting us both.

'He—he had a scheme but it needed more labour than the
warriors themselves could supply. Ultimately he desired to
build a vessel that would travel through space. He wished to
find a new sun that had not grown old. It was a stupid scheme.
We have the knowledge for building such a ship, but we do not
know how to power it or how long it would take to travel to
another sun. Belphig would believe none of this. He felt that if
he tortured me and my people long enough we would eventually
reveal everything to him. He is insane.'

'Aye,' I said, 'and his insanity has caused much grief on this
already grieving planet.'

She moaned. 'My eyes—I cannot see . . .'

I hauled her out of the seat and climbed in myself, grasping
the crystal rod and keeping the craft on course.

'So you conjured up the Black Sword,' I said. 'And the
chalice of gold. And did you send those dreams to plague me?'

'I—I sent no—dreams . . .'

'I thought not. I do not believe you understand everything

you have been doing, my lady. You used the legend and you used me. But I believe that the Black Sword—or whatever power controls it—has used us both. Do you know of Tanelorn?'

'I know where it is said to be.'

'Where is that?'

'At the centre of what we call the "multiverse"—the infinite matrices—universe upon universe, each divided from the other. But there is a centre, it is said—a hub about which these universes revolve. The hub is a planet, some think, and that planet is mirrored in many of the other worlds. This Earth is one version. The Earth you came from is another—and so on. And Tanelorn is mirrored elsewhere—but with one difference, it does not change. It does not decay as the other worlds decay. Tanelorn, like you, Sir Hero, is eternal.'

'And how may I find Tanelorn and the powers who rule there?'

'I know not. You must seek that information elsewhere.'

'I may never find it.'

The conversation had exhausted her and I, too, was seriously feeling the effects of the poison radiation. I was bitterly disappointed for, though I had discovered something more, I still had not all the information I had hoped for.

'Tell me what the chalice is,' I said weakly. But she had fainted. Unless we reached the Scarlet Fjord soon, there would be little point in seeking more information.

Then, at last, I saw the mountains ahead and I pulled back the lever to increase the aircraft's height for I intended to fly all the way to the Scarlet Fjord and that was still a good distance away on the other side of the range.

We passed into a bank of thick, brown cloud and I felt salty moisture on my face. I could see only a short distance ahead and I prayed I had taken the vessel up high enough to avoid the highest crags. If not, then we should crash and be killed instantly.

I fought to keep my vision clear and rid my head of dizziness, my body of its ache. If I lost control of the craft we were bound to go into the side of a mountain.

Then came a break in the cloud.

I saw the dark, brooding sea below me.

We had overshot the fjord.

Quickly I turned the craft and decreased height.

Within moments I saw the bishop's great fleet below.

I fought against the nausea and the dizziness engulfing me. I circled down and saw that Belphig stood on the top deck of the largest ship. He was talking to two tall Silver Warriors but looked up in astonishment when he saw my craft.

'Urlik!' he screamed. Then he laughed. 'Do you think you can save your friends with that little flying boat? A third of them are dead of starvation already. The rest are too weak to resist us. We are just about to sail into the fjord. Bladrak was the last to resist. Now the world is mine.'

I turned and tried to revive the Silver Queen She moaned and stirred but I could not arouse her. I lifted her upright as best I could in my own weakened condition and I showed her to Belphig.

Then the air chariot began to lose height as I could control it no longer.

In a moment, I knew, I would be swallowed by that salt-thick sea.

But now a new sound came to my ears and I forced my head around to see Bladrak's boats emerging from the gap between the cliffs.

Despairing of my help, Bladrak had decided to die fighting.

I tried to call out, to tell him there was no need, but the boat had hit the water and was skidding over the surface towards the looming shape of one of the ships of Belphig's fleet.

I managed to turn the craft a little, but we crashed into a paddle with a mighty crash, the air chariot overturned and the Silver Queen and myself were plunged into the thick water.

There were other sounds of confusion. I heard a shout and saw something drop from the side of the ship. Then the water entered my mouth and I knew I was drowning.

A moment later something seized me and dragged me from the ocean. I gasped. I was in the hands of one of the Silver Warriors. But he was smiling at me—he was virtually grinning. He pointed. Near by the Silver Queen was reviving. He knew I had rescued her.

We were on a raft that must have been flung overboard the moment we crashed. And now they were hauling the raft up the side of the ship. From high above a querulous voice was screaming.

We had crashed into Belphig's flagship.

122

I let the Silver Warriors help me to my feet when we reached the deck.

I looked up.

Belphig looked down.

He knew he was beaten, that the men from Moon would no longer follow him.

And he laughed.

I found myself laughing back.

I drew my Black Sword, still laughing. He drew his own sword and chuckled. I ducked my head and entered the door and began to climb the staircase that wound through the levels of the deck until I emerged on the top one and faced him.

He knew he was going to die. The thought had turned him quite mad.

I could not kill him then. I had killed too much. He was harmless now. I would spare him.

But the Black Sword thought otherwise. As I made to sheath the blade it turned in my hand, flung my arm back.

Belphig screamed and raised his sword to defend himself from the imminent blow. I tried to stop the Black Sword from falling.

But fall it did.

It was inevitable.

It sheared through Belphig's sword, then it paused as the bishop wept and stared at it. Then, my hands still round its hilt, it drew itself back and plunged itself deep into his fat, painted body.

Belphig shivered and his carmined lips fluttered. A strange intelligence entered his eyes. He screwed up his decorated eyes and tears fell down his rouged cheeks.

I think he died then. I hoped that he had.

Aboard the big ships the Silver Warriors were handing out food to the men who had sailed from the Scarlet Fjord expecting to be killed.

From below the Silver Queen called to me and I saw that she had Bladrak aboard. He was thin, but he still had his swagger as he hailed me.

'You have saved us all, Sir Champion.'

I smiled bitterly. 'All but myself,' I said. I climbed back down the staircase until I stood on the lowest deck. The Silver Queen was talking with her men whose faces were full of joy now that she was safe.

She turned to me. 'You have earned the undying loyalty of my people,' she said.

I was unimpressed. I was weary. And, oh, how I needed my Ermizhad.

I had thought that if I followed my fate, if I took up the Black Sword, then at least I would have a chance of being reunited with her.

But it seemed this was not to be.

And still I did not understand all of the prophecy concerning the Black Sword.

The Blade of the Sword has the Blood of the Sun ...

Bladrak clapped me on the back. 'We are going to feast, Count Urlik. We are going to celebrate. The Silver Warriors and their lovely Queen are to be our guests in the Scarlet Fjord!'

I looked hard at the Silver Queen. 'What has the chalice to do with me?' I said firmly, not replying to Bladrak.

'I am not sure ...'

'You must tell me what you do know,' I said, 'or I will kill you with the Black Sword. You have unleashed forces you do not understand. You have tampered with destinies. You have brought great grief upon me, O Queen in Silver. And still, I think, you do not understand. You sought to save a few lives on a dying planet by scheming to call the Eternal Champion. It suited those forces of destiny which control me to help you in your scheme. But I do not thank you for it—not with this hell-sword hanging from me—this thing I thought myself rid of!'

She stepped back, the smile fading, and Bladrak looked grim.

'You have used me,' I said, 'and now you celebrate. But what of me? What have I to celebrate? Where am I to go now?'

And then I stopped, angered at my own self-pity. I turned away, for I was weeping.

The Scarlet Fjord rang with merriment. Women danced along the quays, men roared out songs. Even the Silver Warriors seemed lusty in comparison with their former demeanour.

But I stood on the deck of the great sea-chariot and I talked with the Silver Queen.

We were alone. Bladrak and the rest were joining in the merry making.

'What is the golden chalice?' I said. 'What do you mean by using it to such a petty end ...'

'I do not think the end petty ...'

'How did you gain the power to use the chalice?'

'There were dreams,' she said, 'and voices in the dreams. Much of what I did was in a trance.'

I looked at her with sympathy then. I had known the kind of dreams she described.

'You were told to call the chalice as you were told to call the Black Sword?'

'Aye.'

'And you do not know what the chalice is or why it makes that sound?'

'The legend said that the chalice is meant to hold the blood of the sun. When that blood is poured into it, the chalice will take it to the sun and the sun will come to life again.'

'Superstition,' I said. 'A folk tale.'

'Possibly.' She was subdued. I had shamed her. Now I felt sorry for my outburst.

'Why does the chalice scream?'

'It calls for the blood,' she murmured.

'And where is that blood?' Suddenly I looked down at my sword and grasped the hilt. 'The Blade of the Sword has the Blood of the Sun!' I frowned. 'Can you summon the chalice again?'

'Aye—but not here.'

'Where?'

'Out there,' she said, pointing beyond the mountains. 'On the ice.'

'Will you come with me to the ice—now?'

'I owe you that.'

'This may be to your benefit, not mine.'

CHAPTER FOUR

THE KNIFE AND THE CUP

The Silver Queen and the Eternal Champion were two weeks departed from the Scarlet Fjord. They had gone in a boat which had taken them to deserted Rowernarc. They had sought the chariot in which the Eternal Champion had come to Rowernarc. They found it. They fed the beasts that pulled the chariot and then they climbed into it and were borne through the mountains, out to the plains of the South Ice.

Now the Silver Queen and the Eternal Champion stood surrounded on all sides by ice and a wind came up and blew our cloaks about our bodies as we stared up at the small red sun.

'You affected many destinies when you chose to summon me,' I said.

She shivered. 'I know,' she said.

'And now we must fulfil the whole prophecy,' I said. 'The whole of it.'

'If that will free you, Champion.'

'It might bring me an inch nearer to that which I desire,' I told her. 'No more. We deal in cosmic matters, Silver Queen.'

'Are we only pawns, Sir Champion? Can we control nothing of that destiny?'

'Precious little, queen.'

She sighed and spread her arms, turning her face to the brooding sky. 'I summon the Screaming Chalice!' she cried.

I unsheathed the Black Sword and I stood with it point first in the ice, my two hands gripping the two halves of the crosspiece.

The Black Sword began to tremble and it began to sing.

'I summon the Screaming Chalice!' the Queen of Moon cried again.

The Black Sword shuddered in my grasp.

Now tears fell down the Silver Queen's silver cheeks and she fell to her knees on the ice.

The wind blew stronger. It came from nowhere. It was not a natural wind.

For the third time she called: 'I summon the Screaming Chalice!'

I raised the Black Sword—or it dragged my hands behind it—and almost tenderly I plunged the blade into her back as she lay spread-eagled on the ice. I had slain her in this manner so that I should not see her face.

Her body writhed. She groaned and then she screamed and her voice blended with the moan of the wind, with the howling of the sword, with my cries of anguish and then, at last, with the shrill whine that grew so that it drowned all other sound.

And the Screaming Chalice stood upon the ice, blinding me with its radiance. I flung one hand over my eyes and felt the Black Sword leave my grasp.

When I looked again I saw that the huge sword was hovering over the chalice.

And from it poured blood.

Blood ran down the black blade and flooded into the chalice, and when the chalice was full the Black Sword fell to the ice.

And it seemed to me then—although I could not swear this happened—that a huge hand reached down from the faded sky and picked up the chalice and drew it higher and higher into the air until it vanished.

And then I saw a crimson aura spring around the sun. It flickered and was hardly visible at first, but then it grew brighter and the twilight turned to late afternoon and I knew that soon it would be morning again.

Do not ask me how this came to pass—how time itself was turned back. I have been many heroes on many worlds, but I do not believe I have ever witnessed another event as strange and terrifying as that which took place on the South Ice after the Black Sword slew the Silver Queen.

The prophecy was complete. It had been my fate to bring death to this dying world—and now life.

I thought of the Black Sword differently then. It had done much that was evil in my eyes, but perhaps the evil had been to accomplish a greater good.

I walked to where it had fallen. I stooped to pick it up.

But the sword had gone. Only its shadow was left on the ice.

I removed the scabbard from my belt and put it near that shadow. I walked back to where I had left my chariot and I climbed into it.

I looked at the corpse of the Silver Queen, stretched where I had slain her. To save her people she had conjured up cosmic forces of indescribable power. And those forces had brought about her death.

'Would that they had brought about mine,' I murmured as the chariot's wheels began to roll.

I did not expect to be much longer on the South Ice. Soon, I knew, I would be called again. And when I was called I would try once more to find my way back to Ermizhad, my Eldren princess. I would look for Tanelorn—eternal Tanelorn—and one day, perhaps, I would know peace again.